The Dragon that Guards the Center

By J D Wallace

For Carolyn, and the girls.

For your inspiration and affection.

This is a work of fiction. All characters and events are imaginary. They are not meant to represent or be taken as commentary on any real persons or events

Published 2015 by JD Wallace

Through Createspace

Books by J D Wallace

The Boarder series

The Boarder

The Dragon That Guards The Center

A Lion At The Gate Of The Temple (winter 2015)

Cat From The Second World (spring 2016)

Science fiction

Lucky Star series

Jade (summer 2016)

A lucky Star (fall 2016)

Poetry

Rhyming Words with Carolyn Chau

Chapter 1 Dry Air

The air was dry. I could feel the moisture in my skin being leached away by the thin air. Even my breathing felt labored. As each breath left me more of that vital water was wasted. There was nothing I could think of that satisfied me more than the thought of another drink from my half empty water bottle. The day was not even half over and I would need to conserve to make it back to Albuquerque.

I was several miles out to the southwest of the nearest neighborhoods. At the rate I was walking it would take me another four or five hours.

I walked along the dirt road hoping someone would stop and offer a ride. I hadn't counted on the reception I'd gotten on the reservation. They were not at all receptive of my purpose for being there. At first I was simply mystified at the attitude. Then the realization came to me that he had no desire to listen to what I had to say. The fact that I didn't find any sign of corruption, or the open gate that I thought I would, caused me even more concern. I really felt I had it right this time. The lens was harder to use than I'd thought. And now I was stuck walking from the edge of the LA Guero Pueblo back toward I-40. According to my best guess I was about 12 miles away. I was hoping to get a ride back to the city once I got to the interstate.

The hot sun and the altitude were playing havoc with my body and it felt hotter than it probably was. I wish I'd brought a hat to shade away the sun from my face. At least the sunglasses kept my eyes from being overwhelmed by the reflections of light off the dry sandy ground.

Small bushes and ever present cacti dotted the landscape. Occasionally the wind wound up and tumbleweeds would roll across the landscape. Sometimes the wind blasted particles of sand at me, stinging me with its blistering heat.

I suppose I should have felt lucky I decided to wear sneakers and jeans instead of going for a more formal suit and tie. The polo was a bit of a problem though as my arms were showing signs of sunburn.

The last several months had been a long list of failures to find any new information regarding the potential open gateway. I'd traveled by train and bus across the northeast, then west from Virginia. Each time I used the lens I thought I was getting closer to my destination. So far I was coming up empty.

I told myself that I'd head back and try to convince Grieta to give me more information, after the failure here in New Mexico. Somehow that didn't set well with me. I was not used to failing at anything. Knowing that I had limited time to accomplish my goal, I felt that heading back would be a waste of valuable time. Really, the last several months seemed to have been wasted.

I suppose I should start by reviewing a little of what happened so far. After all, you may not be able to read these journals in order and I should try to make each one as complete as possible.

A few months ago I'd come across a gateway that could be used to travel to other worlds. To say it was a gateway might not be accurate but that is the simple way to describe it. The gateway is a sentient entity which I named Grieta. This being had been a source of help as well as information about the enemy we face. It was also something of a hindrance. Somehow I'd managed to make it a friend of sorts. Since then it had helped us detect, then destroy a corruption that had killed several friends and threatened to bring over more corruption.

Maria, James, and I were the only survivors of the event and we had been working to discover an open gate somewhere near the one Maria's family had been guarding.

The Drakson family came to the new world as part of the pilgrim movement to avoid persecution. Through mutual need they became integrated with the local Manandan tribe. It was then that they discovered the gate and its terrible secret. The stoic Calvinism which they fallowed made them perfect for the task of watching and recording the history of the next several hundred years.

When I met them, their father had just been performing a special ritual which was supposed to allow him to detect an open gateway nearby. He succumbed to the corruption and began murdering his children one by one.

Only by luck had the three of us survived. In the end I was now carrying a form of corruption that would eventually kill me. This infection of the soul gave me the unusual side effect of being able to detect a corrupted creature.

As a group, Maria and James and I had determined we should seek out the open gate and set up watch on it or close it if possible. Grieta was not happy on that account as the gates were in effect part of it. Really, to Grieta, all the gates were the same location. In our world they resolved into different locations simply because the physics in our universe doesn't allow for coincident locations. That is to say the same particle of matter cannot occupy the exact location of another particle even if in all other ways it is identical. I know there are physicists out there that will say that isn't exactly true but the allegory is close enough for most laymen.

The thing that has been bothering me for the last several months is when the Gateway says something is close, it could mean a few miles or half a world away. There really is no telling. I was also beginning to realize that direction was something of a challenge as the gateways essentially existed in only a single dimension of space, basically length but no height or width. With only length as a reference it was very difficult to get anything other than a general direction.

Zack had created a lozenge shaped stone that would act as both a lock and a lens. It would hopefully allow me to find the other gate and by use of several spells, to lock access of it off from the other side. Since he was killed right after he created it, the instruction to use it had not been clearly given. All we knew of its operation came from a single note he left and several hours of research. I occasionally called Maria to see if she had any new information, but so far there was not much she could do to help.

I'd discovered one creature since, and it took a great deal of effort to destroy it.

So here I was, walking on a dirt road in the summer heat of New Mexico. Even though I'd been sweating, the dry air evaporated it away so quickly that only white rings of salt showed on my clothing.

I lost my cell phone and my watch when I'd been forced to evacuate the reservation in a hurry. The successive flight also resulted in several scrapes, some tears in my jeans, and a small offering of cactus needles in the palm of my left hand. I continued to try to bite the needles out as I walked along the road but so far success had eluded me. Several very small needles seemed inclined to stay in my hand. They stuck out almost like fur. A little rash was developing around the area of trauma.

In all though, I was lucky to have made off as well as I had. As I sprinted away from the offered danger I slipped behind a large old pick-up. In the bed of the truck, a dozen large bottles of water seemed to have been dumped. I reached in and grabbed one as I heard the distinctive sound of the brake action shotgun being closed.

Wasting no more time I fled to the side of the road and into a ditch that ran alongside. This was where I'd picked up the cactus needles. I ran along the bottom of the ditch for a mile or so. There was no sign of being followed, so I cautiously climbed up and continued along the road. I reached into my pocket for my phone and found that I'd lost it along the way, maybe in the ditch. The phone I could replace if I got back to town. I remembered my watch snapping off as I flew down the side of the ditch. It wasn't an expensive piece so I didn't go after it.

I had walked at least eight miles since then and the sun and heat had begun to take its toll.

I sensed the approach of a car behind me on the road. I stepped to the side and attempted to wave it down. The young man jammed his hand into the horn then sped by leaving a cloud of dust and sand which blasted into my lungs and eyes. I almost laughed at my misfortune. Out on the deserted road and the only one that I come across is a rude self-absorbed young man. After a moment I began walking again. The cloud was beginning to thin and I could see that the driver had stopped a few hundred yards ahead. The tail lights went out and the driver side door opened. It would be just my luck if he had decided to mess with me. I was tired and exhausted and didn't feel like arguing about being in his way on a dirt road in the middle of nowhere.

A man stepped out of the silver Impala. He stood about six feet tall and seemed on the skinny side. He was wearing khakis and a red flannel shirt buttoned to the top. A similar red bandana wrapped his head. He began walking toward me slowly, dragging one foot in an exaggerated way. He held his left hand out away from his body and his right was forced down scraping his inner thigh as he walked toward me.

"Essay, Vato you need a ride?" he called.

He was being friendly. It seems I'd misjudged his intention.

"Thanks" I called back.

As I approached he spun on a heel and walked slowly back toward the car waving his hand as though he wanted me to hurry.

I sped up my steps. In a few moments I was along the passenger side of the car. I realized how low to the ground it was. Climbing in was kind of weird. I felt like I was going to hit my head. The front bench seat was low to the floor as well. Even though I was more than average height I could barely see above the dash. He looked at me then did a kind of double take.

"Dude, I thought you was my brother in law. Don't matter I guess. Buckle up, homey."

I searched for the non-evident seatbelt. After a few moments he laughed and told me there wasn't a seatbelt. "I'm Hector, who the hell are you?" he asked in a friendly tone.

"I'm Chris. Thanks for the lift."

"What you doing walking all the way out here?" he asked.

"I was over at the reservation and had a run in with some of the elders." I offered.

"Dude, they kick you out of their Hogan?" his laughter was almost contagious.

"Yeah, something like that."

"Where are you going anyway? Maybe I can drop you off."

I told him the hotel in Old Town where I was staying.

"No worries" he said. "My sister lives off Lomas. I'm going to her house anyway."

"Thank you again" I said.

"Dude I know I got no right to say but…"

"But?…"

"Really, those guys are harmless. Why would they kick you out in the hot sun like that?"

"Well, I guess you deserve an explanation, call it the price of a ride."

"Sure, but I got my own bills man, I don't need any green from you." he said in an indignant tone.

"I'm sorry that's not what I meant."

"Dude, I'm still messing with you. Go on tell me the tale."

"OK, but you might not believe me."

"Those are the best stories! I'm all ears." he exclaimed.

Chapter 2 La Guero

The bus terminal in Albuquerque was downtown just south of the train station. As I stepped out of the bus I found myself facing a monotone world of sand colored buildings. The scene was interrupted by the occasional xeriscaped planter holding native flora. After collecting my bag, I found a taxi to take me to my hotel.

The hot summer day seemed almost to dry. Waves of heat distorted the surroundings, giving off the illusion that the entire world was rippling. The majority of the buildings we passed were either stucco or brick making the sunlight seem even brighter and hotter.

After refreshing in my hotel, I hailed another taxi to take me to my destination. The address I'd been given was quite a distance from my hotel.

La Guero Pueblo lies southwest of the city. Though there is a small town center, most of the homes are scattered across the landscape.

The cab dropped me off in front of a white washed house. The design was from the 50's but the new panel-board siding showed that it had been well maintained. A small porch perhaps 50 square feet was sheltered by the extension of the Flat roof. The parapet cap was also new and indicated that a new roof had been installed probably along with the siding. I asked the driver to wait.

I stepped onto the porch tentatively. There was no doorbell so I rapped twice on the jam.

I could hear the scraping of a chair on a wood floor followed by slow measured footsteps. A voice inside mumbled something inarticulate. The door opened.

A man in his late fifties stood in the doorway, a quizzical look on his face. Obviously a Native American, his craggy features offered proof of the effects of high altitude living. Though thin, his stance indicated a well-balanced person. His dark eyes were both keen and clear.

He didn't speak which made me pause for a second before I finally decided he was waiting for me to say something.

"I'm Chris. I was told you are the medicine chief?" It seemed an odd question even coming from me.

He still didn't say anything. So I continued.

"A friend told me you know about the Rift…" I paused, thinking maybe he called it something else.

"Ahh… gateway? He said I could talk to you about it?"

After a pause that seemed longer than a few seconds. "What do you want to know?" he said in a metered way.

"I came from a town in the northeast where an evil creature made it through. I'm looking for a gate that might be open to them. I came to see what you could do to help me."

"You come to the wrong place mister. Why would I help you anyway?" He said with a dry tone.

"I was given to understand that you were the one who knew about a gate near here." I said

"Maybe. My ancestors have been taking care of it for a long time. The white folks they buried that thing a long time ago, buried under tons of dirt and sand. It was the bomb you know. The big one at the end of World War II." His eyes seemed to be casting back into a memory.

"My Granpa, he was the one that told me all this. They said it was done to bury the evil thing that came over. He said it wasn't just to stop the war. It was to stop the war that was coming."

"Did he say that the rift was closed?" I asked.

"I dunno, maybe. He never said so to me. But Dad told me once that you can't bury it, especially when it's in someone's heart." He sighed deeply then continued. "You don't know what you really are looking for do you? You're just another of them crazy folk, looking to make a story about the Indian crazy man that talks about evil in the desert aren't you?"

"No, actually I'm trying to fight the evil like you." I insisted.

"Fight it? It took them an atomic bomb to bury that thing last time. What are you gonna do against it?" He seemed incredulous.

"I have a few weapons if evil comes through. I also have a way of keeping things from getting through."

"Come on in and sit down then." He offered. He nodded his head sideways motioning for me to follow. The smile on his face seemed out of place.

I should have known by the look he gave me that he didn't believe me. I felt that it was important that I talk to him. I took him at his word and entered.

When I was an architectural student I'd done exercises of designing a home with a very limited budget. I found that I could if I kept things as simple as possible and made sure to keep it square. In other words, the more corners the more cost. This home seemed to fit exactly the features. The living area was only 10 by 12 feet. An opening on the left led to the kitchen/dining area. I could see the free standing appliances and the metal cabinets in the kitchen. A very short hallway on the right led to the bathroom and two bedrooms which were very small. All the walls and ceilings were gloss white.

I'd done some government housing upgrades early in my career so I'd seen these kinds of buildings before. It was much the same quality as older military housing on base, but with no amenities.

The furniture was of marginal quality. The TV was an old wood cabinet which probably housed a tube set. In the top of it, the record player compartment was opened. Big band music was playing almost too low to hear. The couch and recliner where threadbare and the springs in both had long since lost the ability to return to the proper shape.

He motioned me to sit on the couch so I found a spot not far from one end that promised more support and comfort than it delivered.

He sat in the recliner but was leaning forward from the chair. His stern face was deep in the shadows and his long black hair framed his head so that only the tip of his nose was evident.

"I told you the thing is buried." He started. "Been buried for 70 years. But evil, it comes anyway. You say you want to fight it? Nobody that fought it ever lived that I know of. I'm wondering, are you evil?"

"No, I fight the evil like you." I responded.

"Well I learned a thing or two but I never needed to use it because the rift, you call it, is gone. So...." He trailed off.

For a moment he looked at me. His expression turned from one of introspection to one of caution.

"Seems to me that I seen your face before." He continued. "Seems to me that you are lying."

"Why would I lie to you? Really I'm on your side." I was trying. Somehow the conversation was taking a turn in the wrong direction.

"I was in the dreaming before, the spirit walk. That's where I seen you." he inched forward. "I don't go there too much anymore. I don't like the things I see. There is hate and anger. There is the evil one that comes and takes away the children." He stopped for a moment. His eyes narrowed.

"I can see it in your eyes now. In the dark it shows in your eyes. You got it in you. Granpa called it 'The Eyes That Hold The Stars'. And you got it. I can see it."

"No, you don't understand. That was an accidental side effect. I am not evil. I promise."

I knew that things were going bad and felt like I should try to make an attempt at smoothing it over. "We killed the evil thing that came over. And some of the blood got on me. That's all." I said.

He got up and walked into the kitchen slowly. I could hear him mumbling something but I couldn't understand. It sounded faintly like Keresan but I couldn't make out the forms. Also he was speaking in a very low voice.

Suddenly he turned back toward me. I realized he was holding a shotgun. The old design on the single barrel loomed exceedingly large as it swung up in my direction.

Luckily it went off while still pointed at the floor. A huge chunk of the hardwood floor was pelted with the no.6 pellets leaving a jagged hole about five inches across less than a foot from me. I jumped up and ran to the door. Without looking back I smashed through the screen door which blocked my way.

Silently I thanked the hot day for not having a closed door to fumble with. I could hear the shell eject as the weapon broke open. He seemed to be having difficulty inserting the next round.

I stumbled out the door and watched as the taxi drove away in a cloud of dust. The only cover nearby was his old pickup. I dove behind this as he readied his next shot.

Chapter 3 Nursing my wounds

Hector occasionally glanced over at me as we rode into town. I had the feeling he was sizing me up. His overall demeanor was friendly though, so I wasn't worried about his somewhat aggressive attitude.

He talked almost nonstop. This gave me a chance to realize he was a reasonably educated man. The choice of phases seemed somewhat out of place but the general vocabulary was high enough to make me think he must have a graduate level education.

As we crossed The Rio Grande, he stopped talking for a few moments then asked. "Dude, my sister is a nurse. I'm on my way there now. It's not far from the hotel. Maybe she could patch you up?"

I looked down at my hand and the scrapes. The hand was starting to swell up some due to the cactus needles still embedded. "Yeah, I could use some medical attention."

I swigged down the last of the water. "Thanks."

We pulled up in front of a tan stucco house. It had Mission Style parapet stepped at each corner. The slat shutters on either side of each window were purely for show. Vigas protruded from the face of the home about 12 feet from the ground. The garage in the front indicated the home was relatively new for the neighborhood, probably built no earlier than the eighties. The front yard was a nonfunctional xeriscaped affair with yuccas and tufts of prairie grass. The occasional prickly pear cactus completed a highly sustainable and low maintenance yard.

He knocked instead of using the doorbell. The call from inside indicated she knew Hector was coming. "Come in Hito, I'm in the kitchen."

The interior of the home confirmed my estimate of the date it was built. The open floor plan had become popular in the eighties. The sunken living room to the left sported a small TV, and white leather furniture. The dining area to the right was open to the kitchen except for a breakfast counter separating the room. Four black metal and leather barstools were parked there. The walnut finished dining table was almost too large for the remainder of the room. Both leafs were inserted and a total of eight harp back chairs nestled under its heavy shadow.

I looked over at him. "She thinks she's my mom." He was trying to act as though it was offensive but I could tell he had genuine affection for her.

We entered and turned left. "I brought a friend" he said.

As we entered the kitchen, she seemed to be ready to say something about his choice of friends. She stopped as she looked at me and smiled a concerned smile.

"He got into a fight with a cactus. This is my sister, Lucy" Hector said.

"Let me see." She reached for my hand. Lucy stood about 5'6" and was slightly overweight. Her dark skin was smooth and showed no sign of defect. Though she was without makeup her eyes seemed to draw me in. The dark pupils matched the shoulder length straight black hair. She was wearing a pink flowered nurse's uniform that almost seemed more like pajamas.

There was a first aid kit mounted on the wall next to a sliding glass door that led to the backyard. I looked out over the area as she began to pick out the needles with a pair of tweezers.

The yard had lawn, mowed close and very lush. There was also a brick patio with wrought iron furniture. A Russian olive and a cottonwood tree flanked the back corners of the 1/8th acre.

A stinging sensation forced me back to my hand. She'd sprayed antiseptic on it. "Best to leave this without a bandage for now. Let's look at those scrapes."

Just then the front door opened and a voice called out. "Hey, lady, I'm home."

"In here Jack." She replied.

Jack was rather tall, 6'4" and somewhat slim. He wore a jacket which seemed out of place for the summer heat. I noted the small telltale bulge of a pancake holster on his right hip. Around his neck was a lanyard from which depended the badge of an APD detective.

"Hey Hector, You staying out of trouble?" he asked.

"No." was Hector's reply. Hector smiled at me then simply introduced me to his brother in law. "Jack this is Chris. He got into a fight with a cactus."

"You said that already." Lucy chided him.

"Yeah, but it's funny." Hector replied. It ain't often some Gringo gets his stuff handed to him by an old Indian."

"What happened?" Jack asked.

"This dude, he was out trying to find some canyon. Went to the La Guero Pueblo and then pisses of the old medicine man. He gets shot at, then falls down a ditch. That's when I found him."

"The way you tell it is more interesting" I said.

"He shot at you?"

"Yeah, but I think he was trying to miss me." I said not wanting to compromise my real reason for being in the area.

Even though I told Hector more about my real purpose, I felt it wouldn't do to make them think I was crazy. The fact that Jack was a police detective also made me reticent about involving him too much in my own problem.

"OK, I'm done." Lucy interjected. "Are you injured in any other way? Just the scrapes and needles?" She asked.

"No, I'm fine otherwise." I said.

"Are your eyes OK?" She asked.

"Yes why....?" I realized the light had probably given away the colorful side effect of my recent adventures. "Oh yeah, natural thing. Rare I guess."

"They are very pretty." She said and smiled.

"Don't go taking in another stray." Jack admonished her with a smile.

She smiled back and leaned over to kiss his cheek. "No problem."

"Hector, dinner is almost ready. You want to stay? Chris, you too?" She added.

Hector looked over at me and smiled. "She is the best cook in New Mexico. You should stay."

"OK, thank you." I accepted.

Lucy began busying herself with getting the meal sorted out. As she did she talked about her day at the hospital.

She worked for University of New Mexico Hospital in the ER. As a nurse, she had encountered a number of minor injuries during the day. She was very meticulous about detailing each without specifying how they came about or mentioning names.

Hector and Jack occasionally nodded or replied with a question on one point or another. I became aware that all three of them were highly intelligent and educated persons. Jack seemed to have a vocabulary that tended toward the legal aspect where Hector was obviously trained in medical or perhaps biological sciences.

After a few minutes of listening I entered into the spirit of the game, asking about points of treatment. They seemed taken aback for a moment then each with a smile accepted me into the conversation as though I knew the rules.

It was obviously a game they played often. By the time dinner was ready, I felt curious enough to ask. "So Hector." I paused. "You are pretty well educated aren't you?"

"Hector is finishing his PHD in Microbiology." Lucy said with pride. "He works at the virus lab just up the hill from the hospital."

"Speaking of that, I got those samples from the wild rodents today." Hector smiled. "That's why I was out there on that road. There was a little outbreak on the 'Res.' I had to get some samples to confirm if it was just bubonic plague or something worse. I'll get them analyzed tomorrow."

"Also I have the report for you Jack, on that stuff you found on the body of that murdered guy. The file's in my car." Hector got up and headed out to retrieve the file.

"Homicide detective?" I asked.

"Yeah, the people in this city seem bent on killing each other." He sighed. "But, I'm doing my best to find the bad seeds."

"We have a real winner right now." He said. "This one turns out to be crazy about brains. I mean that he kills them then cuts out part of the brain. The first one seemed kind of like a joke. Now there are four more. FBI is in on it now. A serial killer cutting brains out. Gives me the creeps."

"I can imagine." I offered. "The whole brain or just part of the brain?" I asked.

"Just part. The parts in the back that are thought to store long term memory and the visual cortex. A small hole about a quarter of an inch in diameter is bored into the back of the head. Somehow the killer neatly cuts that area of the brain out and removes it through the hole."

By then Hector had come in and handed Jack the report.

"It is biological!" Jack exclaimed.

"Yep, it's not brain matter though. The DNA in it is pretty badly decayed so I think it might have come from the tool used to cut him open. Also the cells are suspended in a substance I've never seen before. Like a kind of blood plasma but it also carries some kind of particulate matter. Maybe grains of crystal by the way they reflect light in a rainbow pattern."

"Like glitter" I asked.

"It looks kind of like that." Hector said.

"Can I see?" I reached for the file.

Jack handed it to me with a quizzical look.

I poured over the details of the report. The back of the file folder had a slide encased in plastic taped to the back. It was labeled 'sample 1'. I shuddered when I saw it. The cool coloration and sparkling effect indicated clearly it was from a corrupted creature.

Chapter 4 Who to Trust?

I'll offer a bit of explanation about how I can see the corruption. Before I was exposed, I would see a slight glittering in the blood and mucous of the corrupted creature. After exposure the glittering is more expressed and instead of shiny bits in the fluids, there is a black smoke that wisps from the glitter. I suppose the explanation is somewhat vague. The reality is that it's more of a feeling of a kind of radiated malignancy.

In any case the substance between the slides was definitely from a corrupted creature.

The challenge now was to decide whether to trust these new friends or not. In all probability they would think I was crazy, or worse. Part of my new calling was to track down any corruption that leaks into the world and stop it. Perhaps I could also find out the location of the gate and do something about it.

We sat down to a dinner of chicken enchiladas in green chile sauce. Though the food was somewhat mild for typical Mexican fare, I enjoyed the flavor.

I was informed that the chile was a product from New Mexico. The food preparation was slightly different from other Mexican based cuisine. Though I hadn't had much experience with the difference I did appreciate the meal.

Occasionally conversation drifted between each of the family members recent events. It seemed that my first impression of Hector was pretty far off mark.

"Can I ask something?" I said to Hector.

"Sure" he replied.

"I mean, when I first met you, you were kind of acting different? Like a tough guy or something?"

"Yeah, you know, Jack hates when I do that." he smiled.

"But really what it is, I used to get jumped a lot. I was little and too smart. So I started to act tough you know. After a while everyone just left me alone. But we grew up down in the valley. Atrisco and Old Coors Road, near the old project. Tough place, you know. They let me in the gang just to keep me from getting' knocked around all the time. I think 'cause of my dad. Everyone respected him so…"

"Hector stayed out of trouble though." Lucy added.

"So the whole tough guy act?" I asked.

"When I'm out in the valley I dress all cholo. People just leave me alone. Besides I thought it was Jack in the road back there." He smiled at his brother in law.

Hector and Lucy grew up in a rough neighborhood. One end of the street they lived on was home to a local low-rider gang that had ties to a larger organization in California. Just a few blocks away a smaller rival gang made its home. The result was lots of violent encounters in the area. The rules were simple. Never go anywhere alone, and never go without wearing your colors.

Their parents owned a small grocery and carnicería at the intersection of the main roads just a few blocks from home. Strictly raised, they both were avid students. Because their parents worked much of the time they spent a great deal of time at the store. They'd play in the back after their homework was done and enjoyed the benefits of regular attention from their parents.

Both of their parents were older when they began the family being near 40. They'd both retired and sold the business before the children were out of high school. This gave them enough money to subsidize the scholarships they'd both earned.

Lucy studied nursing. She found a talent at the requirements and was currently the lead ER shift nurse.

Hector took more time to complete his education and now at the age of 33 was nearly finished with his PHD. His quick mind and well developed memory made the studies almost too easy. By the time he had completed his BS, he'd earned a lab tech spot which furthered his desire to reach the pinnacle of his education.

Now he was finalizing his dissertation on non-malignancy forming mutagenic viral processes. The field was recently expanded due to the Human Genome Projects' mapping efforts. His theory expanded on the popular view that you could insert mutation into a cell using a viral delivery mechanism, much the same way as some viruses form cancer cells.

He'd identified several potential methods and was working on getting a grant to do the first stages of real work.

Currently he was still employed at the viral lab where he spent much of his time working as an analyst for the front stage of the CDC's effort. Occasionally his brother in law would ask him to analyze a sample that the ME couldn't ID. This had happened recently on the murders he was currently investigating.

I was arguing internally whether to, and how much to tell them about what I was up to. The Draksons had thrown me in, pretty much unprepared but I was a different case. And indeed they were a special case as well.

My hand went to the pendant around my neck. I paused my breathing for a moment and touched the tips of my fingers to the crystal suspended from the chain. The warmth of the pendant made me feel completely comfortable. It felt as though I was slipping into a warm bath. Well maybe not exactly but it's difficult to explain the effect of the charm. At any rate, I felt like I should trust them.

"Listen," I interjected cautiously. "I may have an idea what is happening but you may not believe me."

"You think that has to do with that stuff at La Guera?" Hector asked.

"Maybe. For some time now I've been tracking down… a rift,…or gateway between our world and another world. This other world is the home of a being of immense power, whose purpose is to dominate our world." It sounded like something from a bad movie. But I was trying.

"Well from my perspective you can't bring an evil monster from another dimension into court on the charge of multiple murder." Jack said sarcastically.

"I said you might not believe me."

"Go on." Hector insisted.

"Well, the thing is these corrupted creatures come in a variety of forms. From what I've learned so far they are usually pretty powerful. There is always some specific purpose to them being in our world. Most cannot live in our world except within a host body. Some are simply a consciousness, others are physical entities. They take control of the host body. A host can be human or animal and in some rare cases even an object." I was wondering how much to condense the material for them. There was a lot of information they would need to be able to battle the thing. Most important was I needed to get to my laptop and see if I had any entries in the family journals I'd scanned that might help me figure this out. If not I'd need to call Maria and have her do some research.

"I'm vested in finding and destroying these things. At least let me help if I may. Even if what I say isn't true, you might find me pretty helpful." I offered.

"Look you're not a cop or a Fed. I can't just let you in on the investigation. I mean, you seem like a decent guy. And anyway the Feds have control of the case now. I'm just the local police liaison." Jack tactfully brushed off my offer.

"OK. I need to get cleaned up and settled in anyway." I said. "The hotel is only a few blocks away. I think I'll walk."

"No, wait a minute. I'll drive you." Hector offered. "I gotta get home anyway."

Lucy smiled and said. "Tell Min hi for me. I hope she is feeling better."

"When I headed out this morning she was doing better. The dang flu is going round again." Hector offered by way of explanation.

Once in the car Hector pressed me for more information.

"Dude, you gotta tell me. Are you some kind of witch hunter or something?"

"No not really. Actually I'm an architect. I just recently got drawn into this whole business. I met some people that showed me what was going on and we fought off one creature. Then in Atlanta I ran across another and helped destroy it." I explained.

"The thing is they can come over from any open gate. I've been looking for one that we think is open but finding it is proving to be more challenging than I'd thought. Once it's closed we should be able to track down anything that came across."

"How do you close the gate?" Hector asked.

"I have a device that one of my friends created that will block a mentality from the other side from crossing." I continued. "The gate is aware that this will happen and is OK with it so long as we don't actually damage it in any way. It seemed to work on the other gate."

"The gate is OK with it? Like the gate is alive?"

"I don't know alive." I said. "Maybe aware, sentient."

"This is pretty crazy. You know, maybe you shouldn't go around telling folks about this stuff. They might put you away."

"Yeah, I've thought of that." I pulled out my crystal charm. "This is a kind of divining crystal. I asked it if I should tell you and it gave me the feeling it would be OK. In fact it made me feel like I should tell you."

"Dude all I got is my sisters St. Agatha charm. It don't tell me nothing." he smiled. "But she feels better when I wear it."

"Here you go." He said as we drove in front of the main entrance of the hotel.

"Thanks again." I climbed out.

As he drove away I pondered his interest in my quest. They all seemed pretty likable. It occurred to me that I had developed a quick fondness for them.

Once in my room I sat down to go through my document cache. The number of volumes I'd scanned were limited and it would probably be a lucky coincidence if I actually had a reference that would help. I checked the index I'd set up for the best possible volumes and set to work.

Page by page I poured over the material. And though I was learning a great deal about the overall history of the Drakson family, I found myself no nearer to a solution. Midnight approached and I was getting tired and my eyes ached. I'd gone through 3 bottles of water trying to rehydrate from the ordeal of the day but finally I had to stop when I realized I'd read the same line four times and still didn't understand what I was reading.

I took a shower before going to bed. Just as I was finishing brushing my teeth the room phone rang. I looked over at the clock and it showed me it was nearly 1:00 am. The second ring brought my head back to the moment I spit out the toothpaste and picked up the receiver.

"Yes?" I asked.

"Chris?" a familiar voice asked. It was Jack.

"Yeah?" I answered.

"Hector told me where you were staying. We had another one just a few hours ago." he informed. "You still want in on it?"

"Yes." I insisted. My mind cleared up quickly at the thought.

"I'm coming around to pick you up. I'll be there in 5 minutes." He said.

"OK." I hung up.

I dressed quickly trying to avoid the scraped areas. Then I headed to the lobby and poured myself some coffee from the pot across the lobby from the registration desk. The coffee was horrible but it served to wake me enough to think clearly.

I stepped out just as an unmarked patrol car pulled up. The window rolled down and Jack told me "Climb in."

Chapter 4 Agent Hatch

As I closed the door he handed me a manila file with the word "PENDING RELEASE" in bold red on the front. The tab indicated it was a report from a medical examination of a victim named Cami Apodaca.

The woman was 29 years old and 5'6" tall. Her body weight was estimated at 135 pounds, but this could not be verified due the unknown weight of several internal organs and part of the brain missing. She had been dead for as much as a week according to the report.

A small 1" diameter wound was found at the base of the occipital lobe. There was also a deep incision in the lower abdomen, through which were removed parts of her intestine, liver and kidneys.

The organs were removed well after death as there was no bleeding along the incision.

"That's an interesting read."

"Yep," He said. "And looks like we got another one. The odd thing about that girl is, she was seen entering her apartment the night before she was discovered. The M.E. says she's been dead a week."

"Yeah, that is odd." I replied.

"Does that mean anything to you?" Jack seemed more receptive than earlier that night.

"I ran across a creature that had possessed the dead body of a man. It was terribly hard to destroy. In fact it killed several friends before we finally managed to destroy it." The offering made his brow knit.

"How did you kill it? I mean, it was already dead, right?"

"I have a weapon that will undo the connection between the mentality and the host." It worked on that one but didn't on the one in Atlanta. That one I had to burn the body." I said.

"We're here." We drove into the small subdivision of older homes near the university.

The homes in the area were mainly built in the 1940's as the University expanded, housing was needed for the various staff and students that were flocking to the area. Each home was of a similar floor plan but offered different features to show some individuality. The main difference was the roof composition and the presence or absence of a porch dormer. Several had stucco sides while a few were clapboard siding.

Ahead I saw the flashing lights of several patrol cars. The road was blocked off and a crowd had gathered to watch the spectacle.

We were forced to walk the last half a block due to the area having been blocked by police tape.

Jack showed his badge to a uniformed officer near the front of the house and we were allowed to pass. As we wandered closer Jack asked someone in a jacket that had FBI in bold letters on the back. "Where is Agent Hatch?"

A thumb shot toward the house.

As we made our way inside I noticed the awful smell that was coming from the home. The combination of rotting human remains mixed with the stench of bile and urine.

I gulped back a gag and tried my best to not let it affect me.

Inside, the odor was stronger. The carpet in the front hall was soiled with large stains of blood. We carefully stepped around the areas, and continued into the living area. In the center of the room was the body of a man. His head was turned at an awkward angle and his eyes were wide open in an aspect of pain and surprise.

There didn't seem to be any other wounds on him. In the middle of the room was a rather tall man who seemed to be orchestrating the activities of the others. A total of 6 people were in the room besides Jack and me.

"Ron" Jack's hesitation seemed obvious. "This one is just the Head?" he asked.

"Yeah." Ron answered as he placed a large folder on the coffee table.

"Hey, this is Chris. He might be able to help us out. I brought him along to see." He pointed to me.

Ron offered his hand in a very emphatic way. I accepted and was greeted by a very strong grip. He didn't in any way hurt my hand but he made it obvious that he was the alpha male by even this simple gesture. I returned the grip just enough to let him know I understood but that I was not intimidated.

His smile revealed a perfect set of teeth that seemed almost too white.

I judged him to be in his late thirties to early forties. At 6'6" he stood taller than everyone else in the room. His dark skin was offset by the nearly grey eyes which seemed out of place. His close curls gave the impression of either Mediterranean or African descent. I guessed that he had a recent ancestor who was white because of the eyes. I later found out that he was African on his fathers' side and the blue eyes came from his mother who was of Swedish descent.

Even in his dark grey suit you could tell that his was a well-muscled physique. I could almost see him having been a linebacker for a college team in his younger days.

"So are you some kind of expert in the occult or something?" He asked.

"Yeah, I am." I said not wanting to have to explain my recent life again. I also tried to be standoffish about it because this man seemed one who worked well with people he respected and I wanted his respect.

I was starting to realize that I might have been looking in the wrong places for information on the gate. Maybe the better path would be to follow the effects of corruption. That might lead me to the source.

An alliance with Jack and Ron would make my job easier. This would probably require fully disclosing everything I'd learned. Well at least some of the major points of what I'd learned.

I looked over the body and tried to have an analytical look on my face. Really what I felt was the urge to throw up. The body was of a man that seemed to be unexceptional in every way. He was neither attractive nor ugly. He didn't seem to have any distinguishing physical characteristics other than the new hole in his skull.

OK, he was about 6' tall and maybe all of 165 pounds. His hair, when not smeared with blood, was light brown. Even the clothing he was found in was almost too common. His khaki pants, blue polo, and loafers were all uninteresting. I suppose that I expected a ritual of any kind to be performed by robed and hooded individuals wanting to add an air of mystery.

Agent Hatch was explaining that the man was not a known criminal. He was a brewer by trade who worked in one of the more popular brew pubs that had spring up in the Willamette Valley in the last few decades. There had been a report of him disappearing from his home in central Oregon about a week before.

I focused on drawing my mind through the eye of a needle and let it wander for just a moment.

A flash of fear ran through me as the scene replayed.

It looked as though this man was accepting to be sacrificed. The room had 4 other people in it. I pushed away the vision and looked up at Jack. He was kneeling near the body looking at something on the floor near the victim's head.

"Hey agent Hatch." I called quietly. "Looks like maybe there were four or so other people in the room when this happened. Look at the areas here and there where there is no blood. Nothing splattered behind those spots." I pointed to each location.

"Yeah, I noticed that too. So is it a ritual murder? A sacrifice?" he asked.

"I think it was something else. I think this guy was receiving some kind of ritual scaring maybe? I think that something didn't go correctly. Or maybe they didn't do it right and it resulted in his death." I offered. Actually I was forming an idea but didn't want to say yet. I'd tell Jack later once we were alone but for now Agent Hatch was probably not going to be receptive to my theory.

Jack had used the end of a pencil to pick up a small leathery piece of cloth. It looked like the end of a soft leather belt. It was spattered with blood but the color looked to be a dark tan. He placed the evidence in a plastic bag which he wrote on then handed to one of the other officers in the room.

This new evidence made me remember something I'd read. I was sure it wasn't in the material I had available. We were 3 hours ahead of Maria right now so it would have to wait. Maria would probably be sleeping now, and it might take her some time to recover the information I was after.

For now I felt like there were more things to discover about the area. One thing of note was the abundance of corruption in the blood splatters. This led me to believe that the deceased was either corrupted or in the process of being corrupted.

This brought to mind several questions which my insight could not answer. The needle's eye chant had not indicated that any of the people in the room were corrupted. This might be the result of seeing it through the memory of another who didn't have senses that worked the way mine did. More likely was that my ability to detect corruption was limited to the present.

I tried once more to visualize what had occurred. The same scene played itself out in my mind but now I could see some of the faces. I tried to remember them in case I saw them again. There was a feeling that some unimaginable force was controlling each of them. Though I sensed emotion, there was also a feeling of detachment, as though each of them were walking in some dream like state. I again let the vision fade.

There was something in this particular vision that was causing me unease. It seemed to be affecting me more than they'd ever done before. I reasoned that by slipping in and out of the vision I would mitigate the nausea somewhat.

As we continued to slowly walk the room in search of clues, I realized that Jack at least was taking me at my word now. In retrospect, my initial reaction to his comments after I'd revealed why I was here might have been overblown. I'd found myself liking him and maybe even envying him his warm relationship with his wife and brother in law.

I didn't feel what might have been jealously. In fact the feeling was more of a sad joy that his life had these qualities. There was this impression of normal in his life. What I supposed was normal anyway.

Agent Hatch was talking to Jack as we continued to wander through the house. The house belonged to the Sandovals who were away on vacation. They'd been gone for a few days and were expected back on the weekend coming up.

The neighbors had called the police when they saw the lights on in the house knowing that the family was gone they rightly suspected something was wrong.

After maybe an hour of wandering around we determined that whoever had been involved in this had only entered the home through the sliding glass door at the back of the house. They'd only left evidence in the living area where the body was found.

Nothing seemed to be missing from the home. The real silver flatware set in the cabinet hadn't been touched. It appeared they had gone to great lengths to leave the home undisturbed with the exception of the bloody body in the front room.

As I walked back to the front room from the bathroom, I noted pictures on the walls of the Sandoval family. One had the whole family: mother, father, and three children. The children were older teens. The oldest daughter was possibly in her early twenties. The next picture was a graduation photo of the older daughter. I recognized her from my vision.

"Jack" I called out. "Over here."

The investigators both came over and looked at the pictures on the wall.

"What am I looking at?" the FBI agent asked.

"This daughter, I think she was here when it happened." I said emphatically.

A look of surprise fell quickly on Hatch's face. Jack smiled broadly.

Chapter 5 Opening A Can

"How can you know that?" Hatch asked.

"I didn't say I know, I said I think" I replied. "My feelings are usually pretty accurate though. You could at least check it out."

"Oh we will." He answered.

Jack began to nod his head in a way that made me think he was thinking through something and was getting close to a conclusion. After a moment he said in a somewhat amused way, "What you told me earlier, I'm starting to think I got the right guy." His looked then became stern. "I'm going to let him in Ron."

Hatch looked surprised. "Think it's wise?" He asked.

"Wise or not... If he can help..." He continued after a slight pause. "This string of murders has been going on for a while. According to Ron here it's been going on for at least the last 25 years, first in one location then another. LA, Dallas, Omaha, Salem, Seattle, each time maybe 4 or 5 murders, then nothing for 4 or 5 years."

"Wow, ok, like a travelling murder mystery tour?" I said sarcastically.

"Yeah" Hatch didn't seem amused.

I was getting a mixed feeling about him. He seemed both professional and personable, but his overall attitude seemed somewhat aloof. Perhaps it was further expression of his need to be in charge. Maybe I didn't need to analyze his reasons and just focus on the task at hand.

"Maybe there is some relationship between the daughter and the dead guy?" I offered.

Ron nodded to the investigator who had taken the leather belt evidence. "See what you can dig up on the daughter. Actually, get me everything on the whole family." He looked at me in the eyes. "I don't know who you really are but if this is actually helpful, then ok. For now you are just a guest. If you see something or think something, you say something. We share with you and you share with us. Just to be clear, if anything goes down you stay down." The focus in his eyes was both intense and commanding.

"I got it. Besides I'm not the hero type anyway." I replied.

I didn't linger on the fact that recently I'd gotten drawn into the battle against an enemy that was threatening the world. It wasn't really appropriate to comment on some pretty crazy things I'd done lately. Those things included physical conflict as well as battle on a much deeper emotional and spiritual level.

In any event I found myself liking agent Hatch. His matter of fact mannerism and his obvious attention to his duty were both commendable and welcome. Though he was an imposing figure physically it was his charismatic way of controlling the situation that I found refreshing.

Hatch was born on a hot summer day on a naval station in Hawaii. His father was a Chief Gunners mate on a destroyer. His mother was a tourist who found his rough charm and noble bearing to be irresistible. They'd been married less than a year when Roy was born.

Like many other military marriages, this one was short lived. After only another year his parents divorced and he went to live with his mother in California. Only a year later she was killed in a car accident and his father retired from the navy to take care of him.

He moved the family to Texas and later remarried. Roy had several step and half siblings.

His father found a new career at a weapons manufacturing plant in Arlington. His stepmom stayed at home to take care of the children.

The high level of discipline in the household had led to great achievement by all the children. Roy had earned an athletic scholarship to Baylor where he excelled in both academics and athletics. A short stint in professional sports was followed by him choosing to join the FBI.

His career so far had been uneventful. He'd been on several investigative teams that had mixed results. He assumed he'd been assigned this long unsolved case as a way of punishing him for something he'd done. He couldn't imagine what it might have been. The truth was it was simply one of those files that seemed to float around the office. Whoever had it when the next murder occurred was the one that was stuck with it until the case dried up.

In any case there was no doubt in his mind that he would eventually solve this case. He'd been assigned for the last several years. Though it had been cold for almost a decade, when the call came in that it had started up again he went with the same meticulous mentality and discipline he used in every aspect of his life.

Because of the nature of his work and his overcommitted lifestyle he'd never really found a relationship that could gain traction. Several girlfriends were around but none that seemed to be going anywhere. This suited him fine since his career was more important to him than starting a family.

The agent's eyes roamed around the scene again looking for something. It was as though he wasn't seeing a thing that he'd expected to see. After a moment he nodded to Jack. "What's missing here?"

Jack shrugged his shoulders. "I don't know." He stated easily.

Ron stepped over to the coffee table where he'd set the manila file folder heavy with photos and reports. He opened, then thumbed through the contents till he found what he was looking for. He passed the photo to Jack.

"Oh" Jack uttered in a low tone. He stepped over to me so I could see the picture.

The picture was a black and white 8x10. It showed a similar body splayed at an odd angle. On the floor near it were placards with numbers. Near the number 06 was a heavy pool of something that was probably vomit. Also I noted that unlike our victim, there was a small amount of blood leaking from the nose and ears.

I looked around the room and realized that indeed there was no vomit, and the eyes and ears seemed free of blood. I decided to examine the room again with the needle chant.

I let the vision play all the way through this time even though I knew it was going to upset me.

The tall athletic girl in jeans and a tank top placed something on the back of his head. A small patch of what looked like leather, the patch that Jack found on the floor. The man screamed as the piece of leather touched his skin. His head jerked back, then forward like some angry bobble head doll. As his chin bounced off his chest, a shower of blood spewed from the base of his neck for a second. His body began jerking spasmodically. Then he fell all the way to the floor, jerked once and stopped moving. The piece of leather fell off of his neck. The others moved close to examine him.

One by one they looked over his body. Seeming disappointed, they all walked away without any further action. I pulled away from the vision then choked back my gorge which had begun to rise. I could hear Jack and Ron conversing next to me but what they said seemed to elude me.

"Jack, you should get that little piece of leather or whatever, examined as soon as you can." I interjected after I'd regained my senses.

"You think?" he said sarcastically.

"Yes" I insisted.

"OK, what do you think it is?" he asked.

"I'm afraid of the answer." Maybe I was not strictly afraid. I wasn't someone that was prone to panic or fear. The more I thought about it the more I realized I'd need to get in touch with Maria to confirm my rising suspicions.

"OK." I said. "I have a theory. But it means telling Ron all about me and what I do." I hesitated. "But the cat has to get out of the bag sooner or later. You did want to know everything I know." I looked at Ron. "So the time has come to at least give you the real picture of what is happening."

Yes, it seemed as though I was about to spill the can right then and there. Jack put his hand up in a gesture of "stop talking" before I could continue.

"Agent Hatch, this is something that is best said in a more private setting." Jack looked around the room as if to point out that there were several officers and agents that were waiting for me to continue.

How stupid of me. I was there getting ready to blather my recent history in front of a whole room full of people that probably shouldn't be hearing what I was saying.

I suddenly got the urge to say something about how the world needed to hear about this threat. Luckily my better judgment and Jack got in the way. I suppose I'd be handed over for mental evaluation if I'd said what I intended to say.

Jack was right. If I was going to bring Ron in on this I'd need to do it in confidence not in public. That way he could maintain the Alpha dog position and I could stay in the background where I really wanted to be.

We continued to look through the area for some time. Then, after Jack and Ron seemed to be completely satisfied they'd left no options uninvestigated, we all stepped out into the fresh morning air.

Chapter 6 Bringing everyone in

Dawn was near. The dark black was slowly giving way to a medium blue with yellow edges along the eastern horizon. The clear distinct silhouette of the Sandia Mountains was blocking what might have been an impressive sunrise. A few clouds near the peak carried a red-orange hue on the lower edges. The upper edges were dark like the rest of the night sky.

"Let's get some breakfast, and talk" Ron was looking at me when he said it. He hadn't forgotten the unfinished statement I'd made.

"My place" Jack offered. "Lucy should be up by now. She makes some crazy huevos." Jack seemed to be trying to lighten the mood.

"All right, your call Jack. I'll follow you." Ron seemed eager to hear my story.

Once in the car, Jack called Lucy. I couldn't hear her responses but his tone seemed to indicate she was worried about him. His expressions of comfort gave me an even greater feeling of ease with him and his extended family.

I've said before that I don't really believe in predestination or fate. The last few months had changed my attitude about that somewhat. It seemed as though much of what I had gone through in recent days was out of my own control. For a while I had bucked against the idea that I was being used by the Draksons in their battle against evil. It's odd because I hadn't really realized my own intentions as a champion of "good" before. Really it had never even occurred to me in anything other than the kind of adolescent comic book way.

As we drove along, I began to ponder the idea of me being some kind of heroic character and reasoned that though I'd done some things that might seem on the surface heroic, I was more terrified than I'd ever been in my life. Not terrified in the open mouth scream real loud sort of way. A slow darkness had been creeping into my mind since I first encountered the Creature at the Draksons home. Now it seemed to be like a very minor headache, always there to remind me how desperate I'd become. Sometimes when I focused on what needed to be done it fell

58

away into the background. Most times it just rang in the back of my head like the after-ringing of a shot fired from a small caliber pistol.

Lucy was glad to see us. She'd already begun cooking before we arrived and had coffee and tortillas ready.

She greeted Jack with a kiss, for Ron and I, she offered a hug. She asked how Ron had been, leading me to assume they'd already met.

Ron's demeanor changed to a very felicitous brotherly tone. Everything was fine with him and no, he hadn't met a girl to settle down with.

I glanced over at Jack. He made a slight shrug with his shoulder and smiled at me as though I should begin to expect that sort of thing as well.

I sat at the dining table and cuddled up with my coffee as Jack and Lucy finished getting breakfast ready. At first my mind began to wander back and forth over recent events.

Ron settled in next to me, placing his cup down. He took in a deep breath then asked in a hushed tone "So what have you got to tell me?"

"Jack and Lucy have both heard most of it so..." My voice was not hushed. I intended to make sure that no one would be left out of the conversation. Maybe I thought Ron was being rude by trying to have a private conversation in someone else's dining room. Mostly I just don't do whispers very well.

"Let me start from the beginning" I said. "I haven't told them all of it yet and I think all of you deserve to know."

I began to tell them about my recent encounter in a small New England town. I left out the name of the town and the names of the family members but left very little else out. I wanted to be a complete as possible and yet maintain a certain amount of discretion.

I told them about the gateway and how I'd contacted it. I explained my dreams and the deaths in the Drakson family. I tried hard to explain the creature we fought but that didn't seem to get much traction. In the end I'd told them pretty much everything. Then I waited for a few moments while they digested the information.

"I think we are facing something similar to what I faced then. Well not exactly similar, but a creature from the other side of the gate. I used my needles eye vision to see what had happened in the room and that little piece of leather is important. Also the daughter seems to be a major player in this. It wouldn't surprise me to find out that there was some strong connection between the daughter and the family there. The creature we fought in New England seemed to maintain the memories of the father and use them against us."

"Also though I guess we are using the word cult, that's not really what is happening. These individuals are being systematically corrupted. In effect they are being controlled by a mentality from beyond the rift."

"I don't know if they are even still alive. Neither of the creatures I faced before can be said to have been alive. The histories do seem to indicate it's possible, that there are creatures that can keep the human host alive. Or animal host I guess. When it came to me, I think the mentality would have been able to maintain my body in a living condition, for a short time anyway. The only way for me to stop it was to destroy it in my dream with the dagger."

The room was silent. They were waiting for me to say something and I began to drift into my own thoughts. I do that from time to time. My mind sometimes just fills with thoughts that need to be run through.

Right now I was trying to remember the passage I'd read those few months ago about a creature that infected a host body. It seemed to me that this thing was much like that one described but I'd read it in passing and though it struck a memory, I could not say for certain that I remembered the details. Actually the more I thought about it the more I realized that I'd read the first few lines then skipped to the next one. I'd done that with several descriptions till I came across the one that seemed to fit Mathias Drakson.

My mental juggling was interrupted by the doorbell. The front door was opened and I heard a familiar voice call out "Hey Lucy I'm home"

"Min's not feeling well I was thinking you could take a look." Hector entered the kitchen accompanied by a young Asian woman.

They were both in what appeared to be their pajamas and slippers. His were of superhero motif with logos from some of my favorite comic books. Hers were pink with small white flowers.

What caught my attention the most was her very striking eyes. Sometimes you hear a guy tell a woman she has eyes like a cat as a pickup line. In her case it was literally true. With the exception of the color her eyes were very almond shaped. They came down further at the nose than at the temple. Also the edge was very well defined and though she was obviously feeling under the weather, her eyes were clear and very distracting. Her face was not as round as many Asians but also seemed to be almond shaped where the point of the almond was her chin. Long straight raven hair framed her face.

She seemed a little pale. Light circles under her eyes indicated she had been under the weather.

She stood straight, in a way proud. I found that I was attracted to her and it made me uncomfortable. Something about her caused me to lower my eyes almost as quickly as I looked at her.

Lucy had her sit down on one of the barstools. She then left to get her medical instruments. "I'll be right back." She told Min.

While Lucy was absent the conversation between the investigators continued.

"So you can kill one of these things in a dream?" Jack asked in a slightly sarcastic tone.

"Not really. The other body was already dead. When it tried to possess me I fought it in my dream." I wasn't sure I was making my point.

I also realized Jack might have been baiting me. His sense of humor seemed to be a coping mechanism. He used it to deflect the gravity of the situation. Perhaps in his line of work it made it easier to deal with the trauma of potential mental anguish. I began to understand him better now.

"So anyway, the dagger has power both in the real world and in my mind." I suppose in any mind should they need it and trust it enough. What I mean to say is that magic, if you want to call it that, is based largely on belief. What you believe you can do, you can do. There are processes which prepare the mind and spirit to channel mystical energy. Key words focus and material components gather and store the energy."

Here I was giving magic 101 lectures to people I knew would not understand. "But magic doesn't have a real material effect. You can't start fires or create lightning. What you can do is create zones of energy to trap or limit the movement of a corrupted creature. You can use the energy to see into the memories of a place by accessing the residual energy that was left behind during times of stress or emotional agitation. You can see past the limited area and look far afield. Even determine the mood of an environment or person. These are simply expressions of their emotional energy that their existence creates. Consciousness creates magic. If you will, consciousness is magic."

"So imagination then, is the catalyst for magic. Using spells are simple mechanical ways of focusing a mind to evaluate the magic and manipulate the magic in the environment."

Min smiled and said. "You sound like my grandfather." He always said things like that."

We all looked over. Each face in the room seemed startled. I was anyway. I looked at Hector quizzically.

"She is always talking like that." He explained. "Her Grandpa was a traditional Chinese doctor. He did acupuncture and herbal medicine."

"Oh?" I was amazed that she understood my explanation.

She was looking down. It seemed she was almost sad as she continued.

"He taught me to understand the signs of evil in the world. He showed me that there were things I needed to know to follow the tradition of the family. My grandmother died when I was very young. My mother I never knew. She was said to have been a mystic. She disappeared not long after I was born. Grandfather was my teacher. He was the one who handed down the traditions. But he said he could not use the knowledge because only the women of the family had the gift to create. That is to create life. To bear a child is very powerful. It is a shifting of life energy from the mother to the child, a shifting of consciousness. A child receives the gift of understanding from the mother in the womb. They carry it through their life and when a person dies their conscious mind rejoins the universe. It becomes part of the whole. To be gifted through the mother in the next generation."

We all sat there in awe of her revelation. An explanation of her family tradition seemed both at odds with the male dominated culture and in harmony with the idea of perpetual spiritual energy. A silence fell over the room as we all seemed to search our own experience for anything to corroborate this revelation.

Lucy reentered the room and stopped. She looked at each of us and said. "Were you talking about me? The room is too quiet."

Chapter 7 Tracking down the Cult

Sometimes things happen that make you wonder if there is such a thing as destiny. Min seemed to have been raised in her family's parallel of the Drakson family. The difference being the formulation of information based on Asian culture instead of puritan/native American. This opened up a whole new dynamic to the current problem. Just as the Draksons had assumed I was there because I was needed at the time perhaps then, she was here because she was needed.

Before placing too much on the idea I felt like I wanted to get a better idea of what we were dealing with. The passages I remembered were in one of the books I'd paged through when investigating Zack's lock and lens.

"No honey, Min was just explaining something about her family history" Jack offered. Then he turned to Min. "Go on Min."

"Sorry, I didn't mean to interrupt. You were talking about the investigation that Hector was telling me about? What does magic have to do with that?" Min asked in a very plaintive tone.

"We think that it's a kind of cult thing." Jack offered. "By the way I've got something for you to look at Hector. Can you come over to the station later and have a look-see?"

"Sure" Hector smiled.

"All right, we got the physical evidence covered. You said you might know what we are dealing with Chris?" Ron insisted.

"Yeah, let me make a call. Crap. I lost my phone yesterday. I haven't been able to get a replacement yet." my mind was getting a little foggy. I hadn't had very much sleep. I felt almost as though I had a low grade hangover.

Not that I drank very much. I'd tried to join the party crowd in college, but it never really appealed to me. Later on during the first few years of my career I'd tried the after work martini crowd thing. That didn't work out for the same reason. At any rate I was feeling less than my normally alert self.

Ron reached into his jacket pocket and tossed me his mobile. "Here." Was all he said.

I dialed the number and patiently waited for an answer. After several rings I thought it would go over to voice mail but I heard the familiar voice of James.

"Draksons" He said.

"James it's me Chris. Can I talk to Maria?"

"Hold on a moment." He told me in a somber tone.

After maybe a minute Maria's soft voice came on the line.

"Chris? How are you?" she asked.

"I'm OK. I'm calling because I need some information. I think it's in the same book as the one Zack used to create his lock and lens. Maybe about a third of the way in. It talks about a kind of creature that takes over the mind of someone. It's like a... I don't know maybe a brain spider or something?" I hoped I was making my point. "We might be facing something like that here." I continued.

"It might take a while." She offered. "I'll see what I can do. This isn't your regular phone. Should I call you back on this number?" she asked.

"Yes thanks. I'll get a replacement phone later but for now this one will work. If I'm not with him his name is Ron and he is helping us. Or maybe I'm helping him. I'm not sure it matters."

I still got kind of tongue tied when I talked to her. After the death of her siblings she was pretty much alone. She had James to take care of her but otherwise there were only cousins and 2 aunts who lived in the area to offer her support. For some reason I felt like I should have stayed to look after her.

It wasn't love or anything. It was probably just me trying to be chivalrous. At any rate she was a dear friend who had gone through much in the last year or so. A few months ago we shared a pretty traumatic event. But I always felt as though she went through worse than me.

"Anyway if I'm not with him you can tell him everything. Or even better maybe get a picture of it and text it to him. That way I will be able to add it to my laptop."

"Sure, I think I remember the passage you are talking about. If it's that, be careful. We worry about you." Her concern warmed my heart and I felt a slight lump in my throat at the thought.

"Thanks. How is Thomas doing?" I asked.

"He is mostly sleeping through the night now, which helps because I can get more sleep. Aunt Rita has been staying here to help because there are only two people staying at the brownstone." She said.

That caught me off guard. I had the idea that the lady at the brownstone was related to the Drakson family but I didn't know her name. OK, maybe I didn't really care too much when I was there before. But it seemed like a relevant revelation. Suddenly I was closer to them than before. I felt like I was part of the family too. At least I felt that they accepted me as part of the family. That was from simply hearing the name Rita.

"That's good. Tell her hi for me." I said.

"Thanks she says, hi back." I could hear the smile in her voice. I felt a sudden feeling of belonging flood me like a strong whiskey. It permeated me, making my heart beat faster for a moment.

"Talk to you soon. Bye for now." I offered.

"OK" I heard the line disconnect.

I handed the phone back to Ron.

"She will send something as soon as she finds it. It will be in either Latin or an old form of American English which has a Dutch foundation so you may not be able to read the whole thing. Just let me know when it comes in and I'll give you the salient points."

"I can read Latin." Hector offered. "What's the point of Catholic school and all that college if I never learned to read Latin right? Plus, I'm the best Latino you ever met." he smiled.

"Well, you might give it to him if you can't find me." I said. "Really though I need to get a new phone and some sleep. I'm pretty bushed. When do you sleep anyway?" I asked Jack.

"When they let me." He frowned. He tossed a thumb toward Ron.

Ron nodded and smiled.

Jack dropped me off at the local phone dealer which turned out to be just 3 blocks from my hotel. After finagling with the sales staff I had an exact duplicate of my old phone. Lucky I'd backed up the contacts and data online. By the time I left I was a few hundred dollars poorer but satisfied.

The walk back to the hotel felt interminable. It was barely 10:30 am and the heat was starting to creep up on me. I didn't get much thinking done on the way but somehow managed to crawl into my bed without my clothes after a quick brushing of the teeth and swallowing several glasses of water.

The dream came almost as quickly as I was asleep. Well it seemed that it did anyway. It was very vivid. And somewhat reminiscent of a dream I'd had some months before.

The mist was all around. It was grey and foreboding. It moved slowly and evenly as though it was the breath of some giant creature. It pulsed in and out, creating volume then collapsing upon itself a little. In moved the dragon.

This time I was not the dragon. I watched the shrouded form of the dragon move into and out of view partially obscured by the mist. The mist was its breath. The mist was a precursor to the thunder, the aftershock of the lightning. The dragon guarded the center of the storm.

71

The dragon moved through the vast expanse looking into each cave, mountain top, and valley. It was looking for something. Its task was to protect the place from those that would enter and use the place for evil.

The center was the rift. I understood now. The center was Grieta. The last dream I had about the dragon, I was the dragon, but here it is someone else. Who is the dragon? I watched as its golden scales slid around me. I lost view of it for a moment then I saw that it was coming at me, the look of hope on the horse face with deer antlers and the beard of a goat. If it were closer I could recognize who it was. Just then I heard a ringing off to my right. It was an electronic bell that disrupted my dream. I looked away just when I would have seen the face for who it was. I looked toward the sound of the bell, and was awake.

The ringing of the phone had been set very loud. I'd forgotten to change the ringtones to my preferred, softer settings. I reached for it and touched the answer icon. Putting it to my ear I asked "Hello?"

"It's me, Maria. I found the passage you wanted and sent it to the other number. Whoever... Ron sent a text back that I should try to call you. There are some disturbing sketches and it's actually written in Dutch. Nine generations ago the Manandans and pilgrim colonists faced one of these things and it was, according to them, terribly difficult to destroy. It had something to do with the war that had passed between the neighboring village right before the colonists arrived. Anyway, there are about 10 pages of stuff I sent over. I'll forward it to your phone too. Be careful please."

"I will, and thanks" I hung up and called Ron's number which was in the forward message queue.

He answered and asked if I'd gotten the information. I told him I had but hadn't the chance to look at it. I'd get a cab and look it over on the way to… where? The main police station on Roma.

It turned out that it wasn't too far from the Old Town hotel where I was staying. While I waited for the cab I transferred the data to my laptop. I brought it with me as I headed down to meet the cab. Once on the way, I opened the files and started to look through them. I took a few minutes to get my head around the Dutch. After that I started to read the passages.

By the time I arrived at the station I'd only made it through one small section which covered the period leading up to the war between the villages.

I paid the cab by card then climbed out. I stood in front of a five story building done up in stucco or exterior insulation and finish. The long horizontal lines of the building seemed to indicate a slight nod to F. L. Wright stylisms. On the right hand side of the building the overhang proclaimed Sheriff's department, the left said Police department. I went inside the left entrance.

At the front desk a duty officer had me wait till Jack came to fetch me. After showing ID and being issued a visitor badge I was allowed to follow him back to the offices of the investigation unit.

The office area seemed almost stereotypical. An open area in the center was around 40 feet on each side. A dozen desks were neatly arranged in three rows and along one side several offices with glass fronts lined the wall. Near the back were bulletin boards with union and office policies posted for all to see. The other wall was covered with pictures of wanted suspects and a map of the city.

Jack led me to the third of the four offices. I could see Ron inside seated behind a desk. The office was 10 feet wide but twice that deep. Two desks split the room. One near the back and the other near the door. They both faced the door but were staggered to allow a sightline from both to the front of the office. The back wall of the office was more than half window overlooking the parking lot next to Civic Plaza.

Ron nodded at me then bent back over some paperwork. Jack had me set up at the desk in the back. I unpacked my laptop and settled in to study the stuff Maria sent me.

Jack stepped out into the main office area and proceeded to converse with another detective over some point or another.

As I began translating, a better picture of life in the early days of colonization began to take shape.

Only one of the elders, Long Feather, survived the war. He carried with him the secrets of the tribes' protection of the rift. After the colonists made contact with the Manandans it took nearly a year before enough linguistic exchange had occurred to allow recording of his knowledge. By then he was near death. He didn't learn Dutch but many of the younger natives did. As a result there was a long process of translation.

The primary translator for the Pilgrims was a man named Jaap Buskirk. Who was the brother in law of Silas Drakson. He was a pastor who had a long career of studying biblical history. His language skills were well honed and he was one of the first to really begin to understand the Manandan language. He spent long hours with Long Feather writing down everything he said.

After Long Father's death he recorded a condensed version of those conversations in the first of the histories. This was later rewritten by his grandson and those werr the passages I was currently studying.

Though still in Dutch, some English had crept in, and there were also several phrases which I could not translate. I assumed that they were attempted translations of Manandan. I'd never gotten any time studying Algonkian which was the base language of the Manandans, or I should say, an offshoot of it. The challenge here was that the tribe had migrated from what is now New York, some 200 years before. This made the language very divergent from the source. Another difficulty was that there was no surviving reference of the Manandans other than the Drakson family histories.

At any rate, I was able to get a decent picture even without fully translating the text.

The Drakson party continued to move further and further into the wooded hillside. They were two weeks into the wilderness when the scout who was a Mohigan reported that they had crossed into the territory claimed by the Manandans. These secretive people had left the coastal forest several generations before, after one of the medicine men had a dream. The dream directed them to search for a location that was very clearly defined in the dream. For many months they searched inland for the location before finally finding it. The area was called "the way to walk in the world of the spirit."

By the time the Drakson party arrived, a series of rituals were practiced to protect the actual passage from evil from the spirit world. This revolved around conversing with, and acting on behalf of the guardian sprit of the passage.

Jaap recorded that Long Feather was not the one responsible for talking to the spirit. Long feather was the one that taught the children about the evil spirits. He had memorized a list of evil creatures which Jaap called the catalogue.

I wondered at the idea of this oral tradition and Jaap's obvious use of the idea of a catalogue similar to the Catalogue of Ships in The Iliad. Many illiterate cultures used pneumonic devises such as repetitive phrasing to make it easier to learn and remember long poems or lists.

It was exactly this idea that formed the basis of Jaap's catalogue. Herein he described, as was told to him, a list of creatures and their powers. Many also had the creature's weakness listed and offered advice on how to dispose of the evil spirit.

The majority centered on the very real potential of these spirits to possess a person or animal. It seemed there was little difference between a living person and a dead body except that a living person could be maintained indefinitely if the possession was properly formed. The dead bodies could only be maintained for short times as there was no longer a metabolic mechanism and therefore no healing.

It seemed that one of the signs of possession was long life. Some creatures could actively maintain a living human or animal host long past the normal life expectation. Other signs of possession were the glitter effect of corruption in the blood and seen in the eyes.

There were two kinds of possession. The first was a spiritual or mental entity controlling the host. The other was a physical creature entering the host and taking control via the nervous system or maybe taking control of, or even replacing, part of the brain with a living creature from the other world.

The second form really caused me to pause. A certain terror stuck me that a living parasitic creature might be worse in some way then a mentality taking control.

In any case the recent war was fought between the village and a neighboring village in response to a parasitic spirit infecting the other tribe. At first there was no sign of anything wrong but when it was discovered that Ahtunowhiho, the chief of the other tribe didn't age, the Manandans became concerned. A breakdown in relations between the two tribes finally resulted in the Manandans being forced to defend against the other tribes attempt to capture and control the passage to the spirit world.

The Manandans won but the cost in lives was high. After assuring that the remaining members of the other tribe were not infected, and destroying the ones that were, the two tribes integrated and the name and culture of the other tribe was lost to memory.

Long Feather described the parasite as a patch of yellowed skin that opened the head and devoured parts of the brain. The hollow formed became the site from which the parasite controlled the host. As it grew, a kind of external shell formed along with thin spindly legs.

The sketch accompanying the entry showed something that looked like a cross between the back of a brain and a ten legged spider. Along the bottom were small nerve tendrils that connected to the host nervous system through the brain. The parasite could connect with either a living or dead host body but a dead host body would not last very long.

There was also reference to botched attachments. The host either was killed before implanting or sometimes when the host had an illness or deformity, the parasite could not attach. This resulted in the parasite's death as it cannot live outside a host for more than a few seconds.

If the parasite killed the host during infection then the parasite could reanimate the corpse for a short time. The texts were vague on this point but I got the feeling that the possession could last a few days maybe a week. This would result in the death of the parasite.

This seemed to be what we faced. The challenge as I saw it was in identifying the infected people and somehow destroying them.

I passed this information on to Jack and Ron as soon as I'd finished reading.

"OK, so how do we find them?" Ron asked. "I mean, assuming that any part of that is true, what does that give us as a way to find them?"

"Not really anything I guess." I admitted.

"I'm still not buying into the whole monster from another world super-cult thing. It isn't in my DNA. Also if this is true, you didn't tell me how we get a conviction on the parasite thing."

"I'm not sure that is what your options are." I said. "It does bring up the question that these might still be living humans that are nothing more than pawns. There is nothing in here about maybe restoring them to their own control."

"The obvious answer is that we can't." Jack offered. "The fact that the area of the brain that is destroyed is the long term memory center means that even if we could restore them they might not have any long term memory. That added to the fact that the visual cortex is in the back of the brain near the area destroyed means they might also have impaired vision or be blind." Jack looked over at me and explained. "We discovered this in the dead bodies and have discussed the areas of the brain that are missing. If we believe what you are saying, and I'm beginning to think I should, then freeing them of the parasite might not be an option or could cause them irreparable harm."

Ron decided to join in. "They were irreparably harmed when the brain spider ate their brain. Not that I'm ready to join the club here. Let's follow this though. Chris, if this is all true the only way to stop this thing is to kill the host then wait for the creatures to die when the bodies go rigor?"

"Maybe not the only way, I think it would be one way. Actually the war against these things by the Manandans gives us another possible clue. Maybe just destroying the rest of the brain, or opening the skull to our environment will kill them. I was also thinking of the possibility if we captured one alive and under sedation, perhaps a small surgical exploration would kill it and leave the host alive but in a state of perpetual ignorance of their past."

"Or worse." Jack pointed out again.

"Or worse." I repeated.

Chapter 8 Confusion

I had come to the realization that I still had no idea where the open gate was. As it turned out I'd changed my focus from looking for it to helping out in this investigation of corrupted brain spider things.

The hope was that this would lead me to the gate. Atlanta hadn't worked out that way though. Perhaps I was going about this the wrong way. Either way, I'd gotten used to questioning my own actions lately.

Perhaps it was simply that I was confused over how to best do the thing. The tools I had had proven less than reliable. I could detect and even visualize the gate in question, and even get a general direction. The problem was that it seemed to have moved since the original use of the lock and lens. Maybe move isn't the right word. The direction didn't seem to be consistent. I thought that perhaps taking readings with the lens from different locations might help but without another gate to view from I could only triangulate from one fixed point. That point being the gate in New England.

When there was no gate to view through the direction was so much less accurate. I could estimate it to be generally north or south, or generally east or west. That was about it. So I'd moved my way southward then westward on the general theory that I would sooner or later get its location narrowed in.

I'd also spent time in libraries and online looking for events that might be linked to corruption in our world. This had led me to question a few people about possible connections to the gates. My assay to the La Guera reservation was a result of asking the right question and being very lucky.

The fact that the gate was probably buried under tons of rock and sand from an atomic blast 75 years ago made me believe that this was not the source of our recent troubles.

The coincidence of corrupted creatures in the general area made me think that there might be other gates nearby. I had assumed the thing in Atlanta was something that had wandered far afield. The idea of a creature venturing any distance from its connecting point made me worry more that I usually do. Actually that brought up a whole separate set of questions.

Why would I even assume that this creature here was any different? It could just be a stray. The end effect might simply be to distract me from my real mission. Perhaps I'd put so much into the hope that this case would lead me to the problem gate that I'd allowed myself to stray from the task.

I doubted that I was so important to the game that I'd be purposefully misled. It was a nice, somewhat narcissistic, idea. I was pretty new to this game anyway and I could have been over rating my influence.

There were other confusing issues here as well. The creature as described by Jaap Buskirk seemed to be able to potentially keep a host alive for long periods of time, possibly even extending the hosts' life beyond a natural lifespan. While this could allow for a creature to move around as described by Ron's FBI files, it wouldn't really help find the point of origin. Perhaps if I had the entire history of the case I could extrapolate a starting point, and therefore, potentially the gate. If the current problem creatures came through the gate that was buried all those years ago then they weren't going to help me in any way.

I also simply assumed that it would also be my task to do battle, if you will, with anything I came across. That hadn't been given me as a task. But then actually, if I was being fair, finding this gate wasn't my task either. It was something Mathias decided to do. I'm not sure that the Drakson family was ever charged with anything more than guarding their own gate.

With these thoughts rolling around I'd started to realize that I was losing focus on the fact that I did have a purpose here and that, no matter the source, I would see through the task just as I had when I started writing my book on old architecture.

Yes I finally had it published through an online publishing service. In fact, it was selling reasonably well for a book that was very specific in potential audiences and probably quite boring.

The thing that was beginning to really worry me though, was that I might keep being sidetracked by these little distracting problems. It almost begged for an organization that operated on a higher level. It seemed that up to this point most of the defensive effort was due to several separate discoveries of the same problem. The fact that our opponent was worlds away seemed to make the job somewhat easier. But sooner or later a united and organized effort would be required.

For the time being I was lucky that I'd found the few people that had any knowledge of the issue. I also wondered at how in North America the Native Americans seemed to have found and contained the problem to some extent but there must have been gates available in Europe, Africa, and Asia. How have these been managed all this time?

Perhaps it was more difficult to travel from one world to another than it seemed. So far I'd witnessed at least two that were obvious possessions direct from the other world and these spider things were at least originated elsewhere. It seemed to me that either finding a potential host was problematic, or that these parasites were not very prolific. Otherwise we could have been overrun without much resistance.

The next thought caused me to have a great deal of hope. In each case so far the corrupted creatures hid in the shadows, and while deadly and evil, their plans were laid and actions taken cautiously and carefully. This might indicate that a certain amount of vulnerability was responsible for their inability to overwhelm us. The more I thought about it the more logical it seemed. Grieta once told me that only the most powerful of creatures from the other world could come here in physical form. These brain spiders were obviously particularly bound to their host even if they could survive for very short periods of time in our environment. Perhaps it was akin to a human trying to live in an atmosphere of chlorine gas. You could hold your breath for a while but sooner or later…

Yes, that seemed more likely. I felt that there was so much I didn't know. I was also a little annoyed at the record keeping of the Drakson family. After all, they were the purveyors of the histories that I'd been exposed to. But they couched the records in a religious context which altered the facts in minute ways to agree with their own belief system. Had they been able to disconnect from that preconceived ideology they might have used more scientific methods when examining the facts. In the end I'd come to the realization that it was their familial disposition which had caused Grieta to be at odds with them.

I asked Jack if I could connect to the office wireless so I could do some research. He informed me that I was not allowed for security purposes but I could use his desktop if I wanted.

I began with some simple searches on spider like parasites. This landed me a couple of interesting results. I found that there are multiple species of parasitic arachnids native to our world. There are also several endoparasitic arachnids which tunnel into the skin, perhaps similar to our brain spider.

If these murders were going on for several years then it might be possible to locate new articles about similar murders. I thought it might make a good mental exercise to look through various newspapers from those locations and look for patterns.

Ron had mentioned that his file went back quite a while. Remembering what I'd seen in it regarding the locations, I began looking at local coverage of the murders and found remarkable little useful information. I was able to find articles on many of the past cases but the authorities had been understandably tight lipped about details leaving the reporters to engage in a great deal of speculation.

An interesting one was in the Dallas newspaper and spoke of a cult called the Familia Aranea using the Latin instead of Spanish form that you might hear in colloquial terms Culto Araña.

This led me to think that whoever wrote this article had come across something in their research that had offered this as a name for the cult style murders. I know it seems a stretch, but I followed the thread and searched for the name. I found only a few bits of information on a very old website that showed a date on the bottom as being edited in the early nineties. A forum on a linked page had several entries in what amounted to gibberish. I looked at the phrases and words and realized that they made up an interesting cipher.

I'm not really an expert in this sort of thing. I thought I'd offer this lead to Jack and Ron by way of printing out the entire text of the forum. While the printer was spitting out my request, I clicked on a link at the bottom for contact information. The page I was directed to was a list of eight names and email addresses. No phone numbers or other contact information was available. But I recognized two of the names from the list of victims in Ron's file folder.

"Jack, take a look." I almost shouted.

Jack slid over in his chair turning a full 360. He used his feet in long motions and his hands against the desk I was sitting at to stop him. Though the total distance was less than five feet, his athletic movement caused me to smile.

His face moved close to the screen and a smile crossed it as he read the list.

"Where is this from?" he asked.

"I found it on a web page that seemed to be dedicated to this cult called the Familia Aranea." I explained. "I think this was put together almost 25 years ago."

Ron stood up and walked over. He leaned over my shoulder with on hand on the back of the chair I was sitting in and the other on the side of the desk.

I felt hemmed in with Jack on the one side and Ron on the other. Both were reading and rereading the list of names on the contact list. "I printed it out for you." I said hoping they might give me room to breathe.

Ron stepped over to the printer and picked up the pages. Let me check against the files. He went over to the tall file cabinet near the window and pulled the second drawer from the top open. Obviously the folder they carried with them was for the information they considered important. Here was a great deal of additional information archived from 25 years of chasing the case.

Ron thumbed through the contents till he found what he was looking for. He pulled out another folder yellowed with time. After a minute of flipping pages he smiled and nodded.

"It's here. Right here." He said. When he looked over at us his eyes lit up as though he discovered a goldmine.

"These two are dead, this one was a suspect." He held up a picture for us to see. "This guy is on the contact list too. His name is Anthony Vilma. But he wasn't a suspect in the one where these two were killed. He was a suspect in the one in L.A. Somehow he knew these people. Maybe they were online buddies or something? Anyway this is the first real break in this thing." Ron was excited. I was willing to bet that didn't happen very often.

"OK, maybe we can look him up." Jack said. "And we should probably find out about these others right?"

"I could try the number listed on the folder here. It says the guy lived there in L.A. for more than 10 years." Ron seemed impatient.

He stepped over to the desk and picked up his desk phone's receiver. He started stabbing at the dial pad in obvious excitement. Then he waited. He looked up to us then back at the picture. Then back at us. His eyebrows jumped as his call was answered.

"Hello, I'm trying to reach Anthony?" He used his first name only knowing that it would sound official if he used a last name. "Oh, not in. Can you tell me when he will be back?" Ron nodded. "OK he's out of town. On a road trip… Maybe early next week. Thanks." Ron hung up and smiled.

"OK let's get on the flights from L.A. to Albuquerque over the last few days. I think we have a winner."

Jack asked what I thought to ask as well. "You said road trip?"

"I just wanted to know. They said he was travelling. I said road trip. The other guy said, no, he flew." Ron explained.

"OK, I'll call the travel security folks and get some lists." Jack said.

I continued to look over the information I'd found and realized that the site was listed as an alternate beliefs website through a large network of nontraditional religious organizations. This page offered links to the main body of the site which was in much better use and offered a variety of information covering dozens of Wicca and Druidic practices. There were also references to other naturalist, and spiritualist beliefs. After a few minutes of looking it over I realized that the rest of the site seemed to be expressing a variety of widely held practices but didn't seem to offer any other help.

As I continued my internet search I heard the phone ring. Jack picked it up. As he listened he started scribbling on a notepad. After a moment he hung up without saying anything. "We gotta go." He said. The look on his face was all we needed to confirm that another body had been found.

Ron stood up and pulled down his polo which had ridden up exposing his lean abs. Then he nodded his head to each side as though he were preparing to engage in an athletic endeavor. He opened his top right drawer and picked up his service pistol.

The dark grey frame of the Glock seemed menacing and deadly. He slipped it into the holster high on his left hip. Then he retrieved two magazines and slipped them into the plastic clips next to the pistol.

I sat for a moment not wanting to assume I was invited. Jack asked if I was coming. I answered yes. I guess I was part of the team now.

On the way out Jack had me stop at the main desk. He talked to the officer manning the desk for a moment then motioned for us to continue.

"What was that all about?" Ron asked.

"Just setting him up so we don't have to escort him all over." He jerked a thumb at me.

I smiled and followed as we climbed into Jack's unmarked unit. Ron sat in the front passenger seat. I sat behind him.

It was a long drive. We wound our way to the east side of the city. The mountain loomed large and tan in the hot midday sun. The pale blue sky lazily graced with a few wisps of cloud above gave the day the appearance of a George Catlin painting.

Jack informed us we were headed to an open field area near the lower platform of Sandia Tram. There were several high end developments in the area that specialized in custom homes. Running between the built up areas were several ravines and arroyos.

Rainwater from the mountain had carved them out over the centuries. During the occasional flash rain storm flood waters ran through them creating instant rivers that would last only as long as the storms that spawned them.

We parked in a lot near a trail head marked "La Luz". Along one side of the lot several patrol cars had made a barricade. We parked, climbed out and began searching for the officer in charge. Once he was located, he offered the tentative information as to when and how the body was found, as well as some information they'd already learned from the scene.

The uniformed officer imparted the following information. There were only two sets of footprints working their way to the edge of the arroyo. One might assume that one of the sets belonged to the victim. The body had been rolled in from the side facing the parking lot. There was a small hole at the back of the neck similar to the other victims, which is why he'd called our team in. Very little blood was found in the area.

I walked over to the edge and looked down the ravine. The body below had not been covered yet. There were several small placards around the area indicating important clues. I looked at two of them nearby that designated the footprints the uniformed officer had spoken of. I looked down at the body again. The body was covered in dust. It was a woman who was probably in her late thirties. She was wearing very dark jeans and a black button up blouse. Her hair was yellow and tangled.

Along the ground was a definite path of broken vegetation and scarred topsoil where the body had rolled down. Near the top of the ravine at the upper portion of the path, a heavy dent of soil showed what looked like the place where the body had been thrown before it rolled and slid to the bottom.

After a moment of observation, I attempted to get my needles eye to help me see what had occurred and found that there was nothing to latch onto. No traumatic or highly emotional event had occurred here in the last several hours at least.

I could hear the officer explaining various points to Jack and Ron. I suddenly felt like this was staged. Not only staged but orchestrated for our benefit, maybe not us specifically, but for the benefit of the police to get some closure on the case.

"Ron" I called out. "This is kind of goofy."

"Hold on a sec." He nodded to me. Then he finished listening to the officer's report.

"OK, what is on your mind?" He asked as he and Jack walked over to where I stood.

"There were two people carrying the third. They tossed him here. See the footprints? They are facing each other and kind of deep. Then down there they tossed the body and it landed there, then, skidded to the bottom. But look the body is wearing very dark colors. It would be easy to see her against the sand. Either our criminals are stupid or they are sending a message. Maybe they're trying to confuse the investigation. I didn't get a sense that the murder happened here."

After just a moment Jack and Ron both concluded that my speculation was a better explanation than that which was already presented.

"We should get the M.E. here and take a look at the body." Ron said.

The uniformed officer had followed them over.

Ron, Jack and I moved about 50 feet further down the arroyo to enter it where we wouldn't disturb the scene. Then we climbed to the bottom and walked back towards the body. As we got back, Jack, who was in the lead, slowed and began scanning the ground. He looked left and right toward the ground then up each side of the arroyo taking one slow step at a time. Ron moved over to his left staying a few steps behind him and did the same thing. I followed closely but let them do the scanning.

When we were within 10 feet of the body Jack stopped then knelt down. He reached into his jacket pocket and pulled out a plastic bag and a pen. Ron saw his action and pulled out his mobile phone and began taking pictures as Jack picked something up and placed it in the bag. Jack wrote on the bag and handed it backward to me.

I accepted the bag. He'd found a large loop earring, made of a silver metal. His initials and a date and time were written in permanent marker on a white area that was labeled evidence.

We continued to walk slowly toward the body. Though there was blood around the back of the woman's neck there was no stain of corruption in it. I felt more convinced that this was meant to throw us off.

"Jack." I said. "No sparkly stuff in the blood."

"How can you tell from there?" he asked then bent closer and said. "Yep, you're right."

We spent maybe another half an hour there looking over the body before the M.E. arrived. Then maybe another hour looking over the area for anything else that might have been missed.

The entire time I had, in my hand, the bag with the earring. Slowly, almost without perceiving it, the amulet around my neck began to get warmer and warmer. The earring also seemed to be heating up.

I posed the silent question to the amulet. "Is this earring important to the investigation?" A resoundingly comfortable feeling flowed through me.

It was hot and dry like the desert air here in New Mexico.

I focused on the earring. Almost before I'd silently finished the needles eye chant I saw a flash of events flow from the earring. Horror followed horror. The woman was abducted near five points, in an area of southwest Albuquerque noted for the availability of drugs. Several gangs made their home in the area and often turf wars would end in violence.

The woman lived in the area. She was poor and addicted to crystal. She was out looking for some. With no money, she was hoping to trade for what she needed. She met two guys in an expensive car looking for someone to hang with. They promised anything she would need. They looked creepy but she was desperate. She got in the car. One of them slipped something around her neck. Her world went black. The vision ended.

"Jack, I think you will find she was strangled."

"Oh?" he exclaimed. "How do you know?"

I handed him the earring. "This." My smile was sad.

Ron had a look of disbelief. "OK. We'll look into that."

The M.E. nodded his accent. "She was choked to death with a thin cord tripled up. Looks like, maybe para-cord?" he offered.

All three of them looked over at me with startled expressions.

"Jack, you didn't tell me this guy was a psychic."

"I'm not actually psychic. I have a few little tricks that help me understand things." I said. I found that the idea of being psychic was actually a little annoying to me.

"I just notice things that other people miss. I don't know exactly how I do it." I lied.

"OK, I'm not sure that this murder was, as you say, a diversion. It was a murder and we investigate. That's what we do. If it was perpetrated by the same people as the other then, it's part of the same case." Ron explained.

"I'm not saying it's not part of the same case. I'm saying they are trying to cloud the issue. It's to cover the real purpose behind the other murders." I was feeling a little like I was being accused of something.

"OK, just remember everything is a clue to the case. We've made some headway for the first time in a long time. I'm not slowing down just because you think this particular death is meant to throw us off the track." Ron insisted.

I found his reasoning to be sound but his forceful personality was starting to show through. A feeling of calm came over me. I recognized him as someone who wouldn't stop till he'd succeeded. This was exactly what was needed here. If he could handle the murder case, I'd find the rift. Between the two of us a lot could be done to battle the evil.

I started to realize that I made no real plans after finding the rift. I have a method of locking it to crossing from the other side without hurting Grieta. What I would do after that, I hadn't really planned.

Chapter 9 Running Battle

We found very little else at the site. There were a few other minor clues we'd gathered. Then we headed to the five points area. Jack explained the history of the area as we drove.

The area had once been a location bordering on several gang territories. Though these gangs tended to stick to themselves occasionally violence would erupt. Unlike L.A. or Chicago gangs these events rarely ended in deaths. Few firearms were used.

The gangs in the area offered a variety of illicit activities including drugs and prostitution. Though most of the area had been cleaned up by urban renewal and increased police effort, there were still a few pockets of less desirable neighborhoods.

After we crossed the Rio Grande on Central Avenue, we turned south on Atrisco. The area was dotted with run down strip malls alternating with newer subdivisions and better kept retail stores. We travelled along the river till we came to Bridge Boulevard.

I recognized the corner where the woman had been picked up.

"Here is where the woman was taken." I told Ron. "Turn left ahead. The next street…"

After the turn I closed my eyes trying to remember the exact path she'd taken in my vision. "Two streets then right, a stucco house with a red Chevy and a green garage door on the right, a couple of houses down."

We found the house and pulled in front of it.

"Is this where the girl lived?" Jack asked.

"I think so."

Jack unclipped the mike on his police radio and called the address in. The dispatcher offered the name of the owner and a small list of complaints at that address including some drug and prostitution arrests. The house was on the police watch list.

"Shall we go in?" Jack smiled. "You stay here till I tell you." He told me.

"OK."

Ron and Jack moved slowly toward the front door. Both had their hands tucked near their firearms. They set up on either side of the door. Then Ron knocked heavily on it. I heard him say something loud but couldn't make it out. The door opened and a small elderly lady opened the door. She held her hands slightly above her head and seemed to be pleading.

After a moment Jack motioned to me. I stepped out of the car and walked quickly to the house. We entered and were offered a seat by the old woman. The woman explained that her granddaughter had been out and hadn't come home when she expected her. She told us this was not a unique situation as she often spent several days away without contact.

Ron asked for a picture and this verified that she was indeed the woman who'd been murdered. Ron broke the news to the old lady in an amazingly gentle way. His tact was superb. And his expression of compassion nearly had me in tears. Finding no further leads, we left the house and travelled back to the intersection where I'd felt that the woman had been abducted.

We got out of the car and wandered around for a bit before I chanced to look down and I could see the faint remains of a trail of sparkling dust on the sidewalk. The dust was definitely from a corrupted creature. This new insight about my ability led me to wonder at the profound changes that had occurred in me since exposure to corruption many months before.

I informed the team of my findings and tried to explain how it worked but I think I failed on than part.

"There is a trail here." I said. "It seems to be stronger in that direction so I assume that is the direction the corrupted creature went." When they looked incredulous I continued. "I can see corruption, well, from a corrupted creature anyway. I was exposed to a sort of energy from one that I destroyed some time ago. Since then I have the ability to sense, see them. I am just discovering that I also seem to be able to detect the recent passage of one of the creatures as well. I don't exactly know how it works but it works."

"This way?" Jack questioned.

"Yes, then right at the street ahead."

Ron decided to follow us in the car as Jack and I walked along what to me was a faintly glowing trail of glitter. As we walked Jack seemed to be vacillating over asking me something.

"What is it Jack?" I gave him the opening he needed.

"I'm just a little out of my depth here. I figured you were a little bit of an oddball. You know, because of what you told us. You see, sometimes Min talks the way you do. For her it's kind of Asian mysticism. But to have you going in the same way is starting to freak me out a little."

"I can't help what is." I said. "The whole thing seemed pretty ridiculous to me not too long ago. When I met the Draksons, they went on about the rift and what happed to their father. Then the creature started killing everyone and it got pretty hard to remain a skeptic."

I had to stop talking because a fit of coughing gripped me. I covered my mouth in the traditional fist. I suddenly became aware of a warm moisture on my fist and looked at it, expecting I'd coughed up some phlegm. What I saw was blood.

Jack saw it too and asked. "Are you OK?"

"I don't know." I said slowly. "Maybe I need to get checked out."

I reached into my pocket for a tissue that I'd stowed. The altitude and the dry air must be playing havoc on my system. I'd had a few minor coughs since I'd arrived but no blood till now. This had me very worried.

We continued walking along the trail only I could see. It was becoming faint as time passed but there was still enough of a trail that I was able to follow it. It led to a car parked along a large concrete ditch running parallel to the River.

The car was a late model white and silver Mercedes. Many white cars fade quickly to a kind of pale yellow in the high desert sun. This indicated that the car was either new or very well cared for. Ron ran the plate which turned out to have been reported stolen only three nights before.

Ron called in a forensics team, then we waited for the unit to arrive. Several cruisers showed up within a few minutes and the area was taped off. Jack and Ron made a cursory exploration of the vehicle and found a few things to point out to the forensic team, then we sat in the unmarked till they arrived.

I sat in the back seat and stewed over everything I'd learned to this point. It seemed to me that my previous encounters had been with creatures that were relatively easy to spot. They were both dead creatures that didn't function like living beings any more. By the actions they made their disposition known. In this case these possessed people retained enough appearance of normal functionality to be difficult to spot. I knew that I could detect a living creature that was corrupted because I saw the corruption in myself.

We left not long after the forensics team began their investigation. The afternoon had passed. We were headed back to the station when I saw something out of the corner of my eye that startled me.

We'd just passed the Old Town area and had merged over onto Lomas Boulevard. Down one of the cross streets to the north I saw an amazingly brilliant display of the glittery effect of corruption.

"Wait. Stop." I called out. "The last road to the left, I saw something."

Jack u-turned the car around at the next intersection then turned on the police lights. The strobe effect gave me an immediate headache. As we turned into the street I'd indicated, I saw it ahead.

My sight was filled with the sparkling energy of corruption erupting from down the street. I couldn't make out the source of the corruption due to the dazzling brightness of the energy.

I felt my mind going black. My vision seemed to be blurring. I staggered to my knees heavily. I could feel pain stabbing into me. I tried to focus and block out the pain.

I could hear Ron saying something to me but I didn't understand the words. I didn't lose consciousness, I simply lost my sensory ability for a few moments. All senses except pain seemed to have been turned off, as though a switch inside was flipped. After just a few moments my senses returned. I looked up the street and saw a figure fleeing. The figure was trailing the fragmented energy of corruption. It dropped off of him like dust off of a traveler in the desert. It left a clear and easy trail to follow.

Jack had pulled over and stopped the car. Finally I could make out Ron's voice asking me if I was OK. I nodded assent, then opened the door and climbed out. I took a deep breath then sped after the fleeing figure.

You can't imagine how hard it is to run at altitude if you never lived there. Though I kept myself in decent shape, I realized quickly that I was not breathing easy. My pace fell off after the first block. I could see the trail of corruption and follow it but each passing moment would slowly erase the signs of the corrupted thing's passing.

The late afternoon sun mixed with the residue of the corrupted creature was disconcerting. I avoided looking directly at the figure ahead because it caused such pain that I felt I would black out. I've heard of people that have migraines that have a similar effect so I can only assume that might be a good analogy.

It might seem funny that I was in agonizing pain, barely breathing, and at the same time running for all I was worth trying to catch the corrupted thing ahead of me. I suppose it's one of those things where I was just beyond reasonable action. I ran and struggled and nearly stumbled but managed to keep pace.

Jack soon ran alongside and I pointed out the figure ahead. Jack nodded then ran faster. His lungs were obviously acclimated to the altitude and he ran in strong even strides. The figure rounded a corner ahead and Jack soon followed.

Suddenly the loud crack of a gun sounded from ahead, then a momentary pause and several more shots. I tried hard to move my legs quicker and found that I was unable to speed faster than I'd been going. My lungs were burning and I could barely gasp enough air to keep from doubling over. As I turned the corner I heard another exchange of shots and saw Jack disappearing around another corner ahead. As he turned the corner he paused, looked quickly, then sped on his way.

By this time Ron had rounded the corner in the car and rolled past me. He stopped ahead and reached over to open the passenger door. I climbed in and slammed the door. The car jumped forward in pursuit of Jack and the fleeing creature.

We rounded the next corner and saw Jack kneeling behind a dumpster, with his arms out in front firing at the figure that had stopped.

What I saw of the creature was both intense and absurd. It stood in the middle of the sidewalk about a half a block away. I had a small pistol in one hand

and was firing back at Jack. The sparkling glow that radiated from it was pouring out in small fountains to land on the sidewalk and pool at its feet. As the pool grew larger the intensity of the glow lessened.

The creature stopped firing as the slide on its small automatic locked back indicating it was out of bullets. The magazine dropped to the sidewalk as it reached into its pocket for another. As it did this, Jack hit true in the center of the chest and the thing fell solidly to the ground, spouting an even more prominent fountain of glitter.

Ron was on the radio as he pulled the car near the thing and stopped. He was requesting an ambulance and backup. He dropped the mike and jumped out of the car running over to the now fading pool of glitter.

I climbed out and went to meet Jack who had stood up and was walking slowly toward the thing. Jack had his pistol out, pointed at the ground in a ready position.

"Are you OK?" I gasped.

"Yep, but he's not." Jack nodded at the creature. Jack knelt next to the thing and slid the pistol away from its hand. Ron was also kneeling with handcuffs in his hand ready to use them.

I looked at the thing on the ground. There was no longer any trace of corruption about it. He was a man in his late middle ages wearing an otherwise well cut dark grey suit. Across one shoulder was the strap of a laptop bag. It was clear that the bag didn't contain a laptop though because it was partially folded near the middle.

There was still life in his eyes. His breathing came in very shallow pulses, as though it was matching his heart beat. He had blue eyes and dark brown hair that was beginning to thin and silver.

He looked over at me and smiled. "Sorry brother, I could not pass myself on. I'll be no more." Then he let out one last long breath and was still.

Jack and Ron both looked up at me with puzzled looks.

"Obviously it can see the remains of corruption in me. I wondered about that since the thing in Atlanta let me get pretty close to it before it attacked." My mind was going over recent events and found this to be the most likely explanation.

They both went back to the business of checking the creatures' pockets and laptop bag. Ron padded the pockets while Jack checked the bag.

Ron produced a wallet and keys as well as several small items including a silver business card case.

Jack brought forth half of a geode. The total size was not more than four inches across and maybe three inches deep. The color of the exterior rock was grey mottled with very dark, almost black stone. The interior crystal was a rainbow of colors. The effect was that the center was nearly clear while the outer edges transitioned, yellow, green, and blue to a very dark red.

I had an immediate sense of a presence within the stone. Then a sudden realization came to me. This small stone was a gate.

Chapter 10 The Geode

This realization startled me somewhat. In hindsight I suppose there is not really any reason the contact point between worlds couldn't take on any form or be any size.

The more I thought about it, the more I began to wonder what might be an appropriate medium for a gate. Does it need to be stone or will any solid do? Maybe a rift could occur in mid-air or in a liquid such as the ocean. Thinking about the possibilities made me worry more about the potential of a rift being available in an entirely inaccessible place such as deep space or the bottom of the ocean.

One thing that became clear was the reason I was having difficulty tracking the location of the gate. The gate had been moving.

I was instantly aware of the mentality of Grieta attempting to connect with me. I let that happen for a moment. I made contact long enough to tell it that I would try to contact it as soon as I could, but that I was not in a position to communicate.

I felt an almost human sense of sadness when it informed me that it would patiently wait. I hadn't before given the thought of emotional context to the rift. It had shown a sort of self-satisfied pride before and I'd played on that to get it to help. But I wasn't prepared to think of it in terms of human like emotions. I began to wonder if I was ascribing emotional context to it where there was none.

Ron pulled me aside and put the geode in my hand. "I know this is important. I can't let it get stuck in the evidence system." He said.

"Look, I don't want you to get into trouble, but you're right. This Geode is a gateway from the other world. That," I pointed to the rock, "is how they've been coming across. I can't explain it all right now but I'll need to use it for a while. Then we need to find a way to keep it safe."

"OK." he nodded.

It was another minute before the scene began to fill with the customary crime scene people and paraphernalia.

Again we played a sort of waiting game for ambulance, other investigators and well, it seemed like everyone from the last several crime scenes, to do whatever work they did. Investigators were starting to nod at me like they actually knew who I was. I nodded back, trying to seem unimportant. The attention was a little annoying to me. I'm not really one of those guys that likes recognition and I don't usually do well in the spotlight. The more I was fitting in to the investigation team the more I felt annoyed. I ended up sitting in the back seat of the unmarked car thinking about anything that crossed my mind.

After a few moments I let my mind go through the spells I'd learned that would access Grieta. I felt it come clearly into my consciousness.

"I'm here."

"Thank you for removing me from that being." I felt it say. "I'm glad you found me finally. That is, this part of me."

"I'm glad too. I was beginning to think I was not going to." I thought to it.

"I have become aware of a concept I didn't understand till recently." It replied. "This seems to resolve itself into a feeling of amity, perhaps friendship to you."

"Um, wow. I… thanks I guess I am starting to think of you that way too." Things had taken an interesting turn here. I suppose that having someone to converse with had given the rift a sense of attachment, a desire for companionable conversation. With that in mind I realized that a new opportunity had arisen.

"I know it's not for me to ask, but can you sense my feelings in the matter?" I asked. Of course it could. Our mentalities were connected at this point. Grieta could and did sense everything I was thinking. Since I could only read its emotions from its articulated thoughts, I expected that it was capable of the same interaction. Grieta could hear my questions and answers and feel my emotional context without being able to read my deeper thoughts.

"I understand how you feel. I know in a way I scare you. I don't want you to feel afraid of me. I shall not harm you." it offered.

"Thank you. I promise I won't harm you either." I responded.

"That is a good beginning." It said. The booming voice from before had faded to a soft personable tone. I felt a connection to the rift that I'd not felt in my interaction with people. Perhaps the feeling of discovery and newness was at the center of it but I also had the feeling there was more to Grieta than I had ever imagined.

"I sense that you have some questions." Grieta continued.

"I was wondering about the being that had the geode. Did it ever try to access you? Did it bring something through?" I asked.

"No. The contact point you are using has not been opened in nearly 50 years." Grieta replied. "Something else though. That access point used to be larger. It has been split sometime after the last use. The other portion of it has been accessed several times. I believe that it is the one you have been searching for."

I thought about it for a moment before replying. "Would that account for this one being picked up by Zachs' lock and lens? Are these two still interconnected? Maybe I could use this half to track down the other half."

Each question was answered as I said it without pause as though our thoughts travelled across each other. The repetitive yes made me feel like I'd finally made some progress.

The slamming of the car door startled me. I decided to break contact with Grieta with a simple "Thank you, I'd like to talk to you again soon."

Grieta replied "It will be a pleasure." Then contact was over. I felt a strange sense of loss. As though I was suddenly disconnected from a favorable dream.

Ron had climbed into the passenger seat and was looking back at me. He seemed to be waiting for me to say something so I gave him a small quiet thank you. He nodded and then turned forward and asked about dinner.

We headed back to Jack's house. Lucy had already prepared dinner and was excited that Ron and I showed up. Hector and Min had arrived earlier and were setting the table. Hector had changed his outfit to something befitting a research scientist. Jeans and tee-shirt covered with a lab coat.

"How are you Chris?" You seem like you are better than last time I saw you." Hector asked.

"Better, but still recovering." I showed him the rash that had developed on my hand from the cactus needles.

"Oh that looks painful." He smiled. "Better you than me."

"I'll take a look after dinner." Lucy added in a motherly tone. "Best get washed up."

One by one we used the half-bath between the kitchen and garage to clean our hands. We then sat in the locations Lucy designated for us. Jack sat at the end of the table away from the kitchen and Lucy at the end near the kitchen. Ron and I sat on the right side of Jack and Min and Hector on the left.

Our dinner was tamales in green chili sauce and a large salad. After the long day I was famished but tried not to show it by eating slowly. Each of us had a glass of white wine from a local vineyard. We also had a very large glass of water.

I was thirsty beyond what I'd expected and ended up having the glass refilled twice before the meal ended. There was still a low level headache running through the back of my head from the encounter with the corrupted creature. As we ate, Ron and Jack were discussing what had transpired.

"So, the M.E. will have a report in a few hours. His finger prints match at least one of the murder scenes. And from our check on him he is the connection between the guy from Oregon and the family here in town. He knew them both. So all else in hand I think we can safely say we finally caught a break on this case. Now it's only a matter of time before we bring him in. I'm wondering Chris, how did you know it was this guy?" Ron asked.

"I guess you should know." I started. "I told you about the family I met in New England and how we fought the corrupted form of their dead father. When we destroyed it I was covered in the dust from the creature. It got it in my eyes and my lungs, my mouth… everywhere. I lost consciousness. When I finally came around I had the ability to see corrupted creatures. Apparently ones that are dead don't have as large a halo as the living ones. The living one hurt my eyes to look at it."

"You mentioned this before I think." Jack offered. "If you can see them, and you only came across a few so far, maybe that means that there really aren't that many."

"I hope you're right." I added.

For now everyone was taking me at my word. Even Ron was no longer skeptical about my involvement.

Min offered some of her own insight. "My grandfather is very learned in things about evil creatures and alchemy. He used to tell me stories of the men who fought these monsters from under the earth. They would come up to kill sometimes. They would come to take over someone's will. He said if you breathe the dust of the cursed then you can see them for a time. You must be careful though because too much will kill you. He had a small jar of it on his shelf. It was all silver and blue glitter. He said he collected it from one of the things he had destroyed. It didn't bleed normal blood. This stuff was in its body. It coursed through its chi center and through the channels of its body."

"I didn't die." I said. "But I did get a lot of it in and on me. I can see them though. It's been several months and so far I haven't had any bad effects." I lied. I wondered if the bloody cough earlier that day had been due to the altitude or exposure to the dust.

It put me on a mental exploration of how I'd felt since then. The truth was I felt a little dazed, like I'd been sleepwalking. Somehow I realized at that moment I hadn't had it checked out. I just assumed I was ok because I was still alive.

I felt a sudden urge to change the subject. Everyone seemed to suddenly be interested in my health and I wanted to get on with my job.

"One thing that is certain." I said. "This geode the guy was carrying is also a gateway. And I've learned that it was once part of a larger stone. Once split the geodes formed a joined pair. Either one can be used to travel between worlds but they can also be used to travel back and forth between each other."

"Now that I have this one I am certain the other one was the open gate we detected earlier. I can travel between them then use the lock on the other side. This will effectively close it off from corruption while still allowing Grieta access to our world. This is important because we really need to have the rift on our side."

"Wait. Am I to understand that you are saying this gateway between the worlds is some kind of living being?" Jack asked.

"Not living as we think of it." Min replied. "To live, you imply that it will die. That is not so. It cannot die and so life is not something it possesses. It is eternal. It has a mind. This is a great powerful mind. We call it the center of existence. It is the place of the dragons. It is where all realities are possible. We have always feared it but Chris seems to have earned the respect of the center."

Something she said started to ring in my mind. This idea of calling it the center made me think of my dream in which I was the dragon that guards the center.

That had been then. I recognized the fact that my dreams had meaning and as I discovered over the next few days, my dreams if interpreted a certain way predicted the future in a somewhat ambiguous way.

Now, however I seemed to be more freely interacting with the center. This did not fit with the idea I had about how the whole thing worked. Perhaps I was starting to realize that I really didn't know how it worked. I'd been guessing so far and though I had no real proof my guesses were right, I figured they were since I hadn't been killed yet. Maybe I'd just been lucky.

Min looked at me and smiled. "No one has ever lived that had too much of the dust. Even just a little bit too much can kill. I know the amount. If you were covered in it you are not just lucky to live. There is something about you that is different. If my grandfather were alive he could say for certain. He was the guardian of the center."

"Like the dragon?" I asked. "The Huang Long?"

"Yes exactly. In our tradition a person tries to attain the status of dragon, to be a protector. The place my father protected was in central China, now under concrete and water because the Changshou Dam was built. For years before that he kept the tradition secret because the new government believed traditions like ours were a threat." Her revelation only served to strengthen my desire to hear more.

"The foundation of the dam covered over the entrance. Now there is a physical barrier. My grandfather came to America to be a school teacher. He taught me the alchemy and sorcery he had learned as a boy. He told me I would be needed soon. Now it seems I have found my place. This is the place where my skills can be best used. It is as he always said." She continued.

"I've heard something like that before." I offered. "From my friends in New England. The Drakson family have been the guardians of a gate for centuries. When I first met them I was offered the chance to help them defeat a corrupted creature that had possessed their father. Over the next several days it killed most of the family before it was finally dealt with. That was how I became covered in the dust. But I didn't know how it affected my perception till I ran across another creature in Atlanta. Now it seems like I might have some lingering effects I wasn't aware of. Maybe I need to get checked out. For now though, we have some work to do."

"You have mentioned Atlanta several times. What happened in Atlanta?" Jack asked.

Chapter 11 Atlanta

The bus station in Atlanta was a long low building. The one story was fronted by a canvas overhang which sheltered the arriving busses from the hot sun. At night it was lit by the back lights which gave the entire area an eerie yellow hue. It was near midnight when my bus arrived. I stepped out into the amber world and retrieved my backpack from the under bus storage.

My hotel was only a few blocks away so I decided to walk the distance. The early summer air was cool and crisp. The walk offered me an opportunity to review my mission.

I'd triangulated the possible position of the open rift using the gate at the Drakson home and Zack's lock and lens setup. Though my mind was sure I'd done it right, this would be the first real test of my newly developed skills using his device.

Maria and I had spent a few weeks honing my ability to understand its function. She also instructed me in the use of the charm that helped the family to decide to bring me in on their secrets.

With these and my archive of scanned documents available, I had ventured out to find the open gate and use the lock and lens to close off access. So here I was, very new to the game, trying to do something which to my knowledge had only ever been done once before.

I arrived at the Hotel which looked to have been built in the time leading up to the first world war. I could tell that the lower six stories were original. The upper floor would have been added later. The lower façade of terracotta was in the early Art Nouveau style and had a very charming flourish. It appeared as though the façade from the original sixth floor parapet had been either saved or reproduced to the now much higher fifteenth floor. The intermediate levels having been faced in red brick.

I found my room on the fifth floor and settled in for the night. I had dreams of flowers of all colors. As the dream continued the colors faded to black and white. Then the flowers began to wither.

I woke early even though I hadn't slept well. After ordering room service breakfast, I looked over the map I'd prepared. Even with my smart phone and laptop I felt somehow more capable with the paper variety. There seemed to be a tangible sense of knowledge when holding it.

The location I wanted was in an older district near the suburbs to the east near Stone Mountain. I called a taxi and was off.

The area around Stone Mountain was made up of a variety of old elements that dated quite a ways back. The scenic railroad tracks and station to the north of the mountain were near where I thought I wanted to be.

My taxi dropped me off at a parking area near the summit ride building. I hiked to the east of the railway station building where a stone lined pond that looked artificial stood as my first landmark. On the other side the mountain rose 1600 feet. For those used to the Appalachians, or the larger Rocky Mountains, this was a mere hill. Its stone face was impressive though and I felt something akin to that which I felt when I'd first encountered the rift.

A trail led to the face of the mountain and I found the area I wanted.

The problem was it was taped off. Yellow ribbons marked with the words 'POLICE CRIME SCENE' block my progress. Ahead, near the area I wanted to go, were several officers both in uniform and in suits. The suited officers I could identify by the badges hanging from lanyards or on belts.

They seemed to be investigating a body. Occasionally I could hear muffled conversation coming from them but the distance was too great for me to make out most of the words.

What struck me was the pale glittering glow of the body on the ground. I hadn't seen this before. I had seen the glittery dust when it covered me and this looked very much like it. I thought for a moment about what it might mean. I felt strongly that this was a sign of corruption. I looked at my hands and could, when I focused hard, see the faintest glittery halo.

Could it be that in some way I had been endowed with the ability to see them, to detect them?

Nearby an officer was standing watch over the trailhead that led up toward the mountain. The police tape crossed near him and it was obvious his job was to limit access to the area. I strode over trying to appear an interested tourist and asked the officer to tell me what happened.

He informed me they'd found the body earlier in the predawn morning. I wasn't allowed access and he had no other answers for unofficial persons.

I waited a while then decided to try another tack. "I'm an investigative reporter." I told him. "I'd like to know more about what happened. If you find out anything leave me a message at the hotel or call my number and I'll make sure you get mentioned." I gave him the hotel and my number.

It was a long ploy but I couldn't help but think I didn't have any other hopes of finding out what happened.

I moved away about 100 yards into the woods. There I pulled out the lens and muttered an incantation.

What I saw then convinced me that the rift was not in the area. My mind swam away to the west, across mountains and plains to a red spotted mountain. There a green edged river wound through the sands of the high desert.

I put the lens back in my pocket and decided to go back to the hotel and wait. I needed to think some more. I also felt the need to call Maria and let her know that the lens was not behaving.

I'd been in my room for less than an hour when a call from the officer I'd met informed me that the body had been taken to the city morgue and I might have a few hours to check it out before things got too crazy.

I thanked him and made sure he gave me his name so that I could get it right for my fictional story. I called the front desk to arrange another taxi.

I suppose a morgue is a morgue. White ceramic tile and the smell of rotten flesh mixed with phenol and formaldehyde. Although I'd never been to one it seemed as though any movie where they show a morgue they show a place exactly like this.

I was not questioned at all when I signed in. I was allowed to view the body while escorted by the attending assistant.

The body had a white tag from the right big toe. It was covered except the face and feet. At first I thought it was a man but as I stepped closer, I realized it was a woman.

She was tall and slightly heavy, probably just under six feet and nearly one hundred and sixty pounds. Her form was not very curvy and her breasts were on the small side, giving her a masculine appearance. The short hair added to the misconception.

I could still feel, see the faint glow of corruption radiating in slow fingers from her like the corona of the sun hidden by clouds. The glittery effect was enhanced because of the slight flicker of the florescent fixtures hanging from the exposed structure ceiling.

I passed to the opposite side where a cart with instruments intended for either autopsy or examination of some kind was parked. On the top of it was a clipboard with several sheets of preprinted pre-admittance examination forms. The top sheet was labeled Jane Doe. The date and time indicated she'd been brought in less than an hour ago.

I asked a few questions of the attendant to try to look more like an eager reporter. He didn't know anything other than she was brought in just a while ago and the M.E. was on his way.

Though I was intrigued I wasn't sure what I could do about a dead corrupted thing and decided I'd head back to the hotel and call Maria.

As I turned to leave a slight rustle followed by a long drawn out sigh caused me to stop and turn.

"Oh crap." The attendant ejaculated. "I heard this happens sometimes." He said to me. Then he turned to the woman who was rising from the table. "Are you ok? Just lay back I'll get you some clothes." His manner was very concerned even though I could hear the fear in his voice.

The woman struggled to stand. The sheet fell away from her body and she staggered forward several steps. Then she steadied herself just as the attendant came along side of her and wrapped his lab coat around her.

Her face was devoid of emotion. She looked over at me and I could swear she smiled. She turned to look down at the coat and the hands pressing her gently to sit. She was immobile. She struggled against his attempt. Then she looked into his face.

When his eyes met hers he shuddered for a moment, then screamed out an ear piercing shriek.

Her hand shot up and gripped his throat. His eyes started to bulge before I was able to move.

It may have only been a second before I decided I needed to act. By then the attendant was gasping for air. I reached forward with my left hand and gripped behind the hand which choked him. An aggressive pull ripped her hand from him and spun her in my direction.

I struck out with a spear hand strike to the throat. I could feel the depth of the impact and was certain that, had she been a living person, my attack would have killed her. As it was, she simply took a step back, then punched me heavy in the chest. I staggered back several steps from the force of the blow.

This gave the attendant the opportunity to run. He was out the door and into an office along one side of the main hallway before we moved again.

The blow to the chest had left me gasping slightly for air. It hit at an odd angle and was therefore not really offering any other injury besides the momentary inability to breathe. As she stepped toward me the lab coat fell away. She reached with both hands toward my head.

I ducked under and kicked the back of her knee as I passed. I heard and felt the grinding of bone and I knew I'd dislocated the knee, probably tearing several major ligaments as well.

I stepped through to a bow stance and switched position to face her with the bowed knee behind. This left me with most of my weight away from her, allowing me greater lateral movement.

I looked on in horror as she struggled with the damaged knee. Her damaged knee buckled sideways toward her center. Her other leg was bent at the knee. This gave her an awkward pretzel of limbs. The undamaged knee suddenly bent in the same way as the damaged knee. In another motion her legs twisted behind her then outward. She fell on her hands then as well. Her body twisted around to look at me on a now elongated neck. The new geometry of her form reminded me of the remains of Mathias Drakson. I knew then I faced a similar creature.

The creature hisses a curse at me. "I shall ascend. You shall perish who has defied the curse."

It then moved away in long springs like a large predatory cat. Each leap covered several meters. Through the double doors and along the hall it went.

I went after it.

I didn't have the dagger with me. My only hope of defeating it was to damage it enough to make the possessing intelligence give up the body. The problem was I had to catch it first.

I was helped by the fact that it seemed puzzled by the door leading to the main lobby. There were no handles and the door was accessed by a push panel on the wall to the right.

By the time it figured out the way through, I was nearly caught up. It saw the panel and jabbed at it with one of its feet. The doors swung open and it bounded through.

The screaming from the lobby indicated that several people were there. As I entered I was confronted with the sight of three officers and a woman whom I assumed was the M.E. standing in shock. One of the officers had drawn his firearm. It was difficult to aim in the crowded area. The room was only about twenty feet to a side. With the four newcomers and myself, there was enough difficulty aiming that the officer decided not to risk it.

Three large plate glass windows offered the thing a way out. It crashed through the center window and leapt away into the bright noon sun.

"What was that?" the armed officer asked.

"Something very bad." I offered then ran after it.

Two of the policemen had come after me and soon caught up. One of them was panting into the mike on his shoulder instructions and information about the case.

The creature was still ahead of us but we managed to maintain pace. Each leap caused it to land in an awkward way further damaging itself. Every so often it would stop and we were afforded the opportunity to gain on it while it readjusted its body, making up for the damage. Within the first half mile it was barely recognizable as having been human.

Even if we temporarily lost sight of the thing, the trail of glittering blood and the screams of horrified people would have allowed us to track it. As it was, this was only necessary once early in the chase. By the time we'd finished a mile we were within decent firing distance and the officers had tried several shots. Each shot seemed to have the effect of hastening changes in the thing's form. One particularly good shot caused the thing to tumble after a landing. It stayed down till we were within a few yards then suddenly it reared up and its ribs spread wide like the hood of a cobra. The skin stretched between to the point of tearing. Its internal organs and intestines were exposed underneath. Instead of simply spilling out they splashed forward, covering one of the officers in gore. The other officer suddenly found the urge to vomit. But even as he did so, he emptied his pistol into the thing's head.

In a very rapid motion he dropped the magazine, turned the gun ninety degrees, and slipped in the reload. The slide snapped forward as he took aim and continued firing. After only a few shots the creature fell to the pavement. The other officer struggled to climb out of the yards of entrails that had encased him. I ran to help.

As I knelt next to him I could see that several loops had wound around his neck and began constricting. The death of the creature had not loosened them and I spent the next few minutes pulling at them to remove them. By the time I managed, he was no longer breathing.

His eyes were open and I felt the corruption of the thing sifting into his form. Slowly the glitter became more noticeable. I struggled thinking what to do. In a sudden inspiration I decided to try CPR. Perhaps if he lived the corruption would not be able to claim him.

I opened his mouth and cleared the passage with my finger. Then I bent to give the first few breaths. After that I checked his pulse, which was still going but weak. I gave three more breaths when I realized he was breathing on his own. His eyes blinked and I saw the effect of corruption fade from him.

He coughed up a small amount of blood then smiled weakly and asked. "Did we get it?"

"Yep." I smiled back.

"On your knees." I heard the voice from behind. I turned and realized the other officer was pointing his firearm at me. I was already on my knees so I simply lifted my hands above my head and offered the best I'm innocent look I could.

He came toward me, then saw that his associate was ok, and holstered his weapon. He pulled his cuffs from a pouch on the back of his belt and stepped forward reaching for my arm. Just as he was about to clip the cuffs on he stopped.

His hands moved to his sides palms outspread to show he was not intending to harm me. Then he asked again. "What was that thing?"

"All I can say for certain is we are lucky to be alive. It was a corruption of the dead body of a woman who was found earlier today. I'm not sure what happened, how it happened. But I think you have destroyed it." I offered.

"Look, this is going to be hard to explain. Unless you are prepared to deal with some pretty hard questioning, you should go." He said.

I didn't wait for further explanation. I stood up then walked slowly away. We had stopped it at the edge of a park where a crowd had gathered. Though several smart phones were recording the entire thing I felt like I wanted to take my time. Several bystanders shouted encouragement to me and the police officer as I walked away. There was a fountain nearby that I used to clean off my hands.

After I left the park I managed to find a bus that seemed to run in the general direction of my hotel. I'd decided that the best action would be to follow the new trail to what I figured was Albuquerque. The vision of a pink mountain spotted like a watermelon was confirmed when I remembered the word 'sandia' translated as watermelon.

I booked the flight for that evening and checked out of the hotel. By the time I'd made it through security at the airport news outlets were showing a battle in the streets of Atlanta with an escaped lab animal. Luckily none of the offered video was of sufficient quality that I could be clearly identified.

My flight to Albuquerque was uneventful.

Chapter 12 The Hunt

A call from the M.E. broke our conversation. While Jack talked in low tones over the phone, Hector produced a manila folder containing the results of his examination of the small patch of leather Jack found at the first murder. He handed the report to Ron and told him, "This is the craziest stuff I've ever seen."

"It's biological but severely desiccated. I wasn't able to get a DNA sample to replicate which is a little weird by itself. This picture under the microscope at 4x shows cellular structure similar to skin but without any pores or hair follicles." He handed a picture to Jack.

"This picture at 20x shows the cells have small pseudopodia that seem to connect to the central feature of the cell. Where you might expect the nucleus to be." He handed another picture to Jack.

"This one shows how each cell has broken open. This feature on the edge of the cell was consistent in every cell I looked at. It's almost as though they were exposed to some environmental condition that affected them this way. It's like, maybe, the vacuum of space would affect our cells. No outside pressure could cause our cells to explode for instance. But the fact that it is desiccated indicates that it could be centuries old."

I thought about it for a moment and recalled the vision I had when Jack collected it.

"No it was lighter colored then and it seemed to move like a ribbon." I offered.

"That isn't possible." Hector seemed to be sorting through something in his mind. "Normal atmospheric drying cannot achieve the effect you see here in only a day."

Jack pocketed his cell phone then smiled at us in a confused sort of way. "The M.E. says part of this guy's brain was replaced by some kind of leather spider like thing. Its legs seemed to be made of soft leather jointed every half inch. Each leg was about 6 inches long. At the center is a large mass of soft material he thought looked like dear antler velvet with small clear tendrils interwoven with the remaining brain. In short, this guy had a giant brain spider parasite in his skull. He is emailing me some pictures and his notes."

"Where does that leave us at this point?" Ron asked. "We have to assume we have at least three more of these spider brain things running around. We don't know where they are coming from. And our one lead to connect them seems to be the Sandoval woman who disappeared without a trace."

"I'd say that so far there has been a connection between the locations of the murders and the individuals involved. For instance the Sandoval household and the first one you took me to." I was beginning to feel like part of the team now. "These things seem to maintain some of the memory of the victim. Perhaps even some of the general personality. It would explain why they are difficult to identify and how they are able to avoid being caught."

"There is definitely a disconnect when it comes to leaving bodies all over the place. These things don't seem to care if we find them or not." Jack offered.

Ron jumped in giving his ideas. "Actually I think they are leaving the bodies on purpose. To cause fear maybe? Or maybe they just don't have a use for the body if the parasite isn't able to attach."

"Well, I think that's it. For some reason the parasite isn't always able to interact with the host. It dies in our environment after just a short time. Grieta as much as told me they can't live in our world for long without a host. Since the potential host is dead it is not of any use. They just leave it there, not worried about the body being found. What they fear is themselves being found. They know they are vulnerable in our world." It seemed a rational explanation so I continued.

"If they somehow follow a basic instinct or pattern of... memory? I don't know how to put it. As though the memories they assimilate take them to locations the host is familiar with. There they perform the oddly ritualistic attachment of the parasite. When it doesn't take they leave the body and move on. We still need to figure out where the original parasite came from. And we need to find the rest of the... for lack of a better word, cultists."

Jack's mobile phone hummed and he tapped the screen. After a moment of tapping and more tapping he stopped and smiled. "Oh ho." He said. "Now we have you." then he motioned for everyone to gather around.

"Take a look at this picture. Recognized that little flat piece of material at the lower corner?" He asked.

The picture showed what looked to be a portion of a withered brain with long multi-jointed legs sticking out and several points along the edge. Near the middle of the grey velvety object was a flap of leather exactly like the one Jack had Hector analyze.

"I think this one was going to be a mommy." Ron said in a very sarcastic tone. "So this thing, what, seeds, the next host with that little bit of... whatever?"

"So now we know. There isn't really anything else on the others on the list from the webpage. There must be something about them in official records if any one of them disappeared." Jack interjected.

"Listen, I know better than most. I can't fight these things alone." Somehow I'd made this about me. I didn't realize what I said till I heard myself say it. I was reverting to my old self. I didn't like my old self much and yet I couldn't get away from... me.

"I have taken on the fight. I guess I'm asking you if you are willing to do this." I sounded less arrogant than I could have, but not by much.

"I don't know what you are talking about Chris. Jack and I have a duty to bring this case to a close. We are officers of the law. That is our fight. If this parasite happens to be murdering people, then we have to go after it. That's what I signed on for. And I'm fully aware that if what you say is true, and I'm starting to realize it has merit, then there is no precedence for us to handle this case. We are really making it up as we go. Our best hope is that these creatures continue to do murderous things so that as we destroy them we don't get caught up in the problem of charging an evil parasitic spider in a court of law." Ron made his point.

Jack furthered his stance by adding. "I'm ready to use anything, any tool to get this thing sorted out. You have knowledge and skills that seem to be helpful. I'm afraid you got it all wrong Chris. We aren't helping you. You are helping us."

"Right." I said. "Sorry."

Jack was looking at me strangely as I spoke. Then he touched his upper lip and nodded as though he wanted me to do the same. I felt the warm wet spot of blood begin seeping from my nostril. I could see in it the corruption glittering as if to warn me of some hidden terror.

My pulse raced for a moment, then darkness.

When I awoke, I was in a hospital room bed. Several needles protruded from a patch of medical tape on the back of my left hand. I could hear someone talking in the room but I could not focus my vision beyond a few feet. The words seemed to be in an angry tone but I couldn't make them out. I was having trouble focusing my mind on anything. In another moment blackness returned.

My next memory came as the last had left. I soft feminine voice seemed to draw me toward… something. Like the song of the siren, it was beautiful, angelic. Not the holy choir kind of song, but more of a wind through the reeds sound.

"You have come to me again." The voice said. The words were clear and calm. "I have waited for you." It wasn't a voice I heard, but a feeling of words that whispered in my mind.

I tried to answer. My mouth refused to make a sound. My mind was held by some unknown binding. I simply tried to feel that I was indeed there in this place of peace.

"Do not try to strain yourself. I know you are ill." The song continued. "You can rest for a time here with me." I realized only then that it was Grieta. Grieta had transformed in my mind from a booming metaphysical mystery, to a friendly voice, to a soft healing song. I wondered if it was my mind that had changed its interpretation or if Grieta itself had altered in some way, changing how it interacted with me so that I might feel more comfortable.

"Yes, both." Grieta insisted gently. "I am in your mind and you are in my mind. "The geode is nearby so then I am nearby."

I felt a sudden comfort at that thought. Of all the people I'd known in my life, to find my closest friend might be an immortal inter-dimensional portal. It made me feel, well, special. I did feel as though we had become friends.

"I must ask a favor." Grieta seemed to be embarrassed.

What could I possibly do? I'm just a man.

"A corruption has invaded and is attempting, not simply to access your world but, to enslave me to their will. If this happens I will never be able to think, feel, sense, for myself again."

Again, what could I do?

"Use the Geode portal and come into my consciousness. I can slow them but I cannot actually interact with them. Your mentality can be active in me. You can destroy them."

The geode is only a few inches across. I could never fit.

"You are thinking in terms that do not apply. Geometric constraints are irrelevant."

I'll do whatever I can. You are my friend.

This time I woke up to the sound of Jack and Hector talking in hushed tones. Their whispers were difficult to hear but I made out that they were worried about me.

"I'm OK." I said loud enough for them to hear.

I did a mental inventory to verify that I was actually OK. I felt no pain. I didn't feel groggy or weak in any way. My heart didn't feel as though it was racing. I was breathing easy and deep. I was OK.

Hector came over and looked down at me as I pulled myself to a sitting position. Jack followed a moment later.

"You had us worried Vato." Hector said. "Maybe you should just lie back for a while. The test results just came back. It isn't good."

"What?" I asked.

"Some kind of cancer. Never seen this before. Your blood and skin seem to be undergoing replication errors consistent with cancer. The blood panel confirmed the signs. It's crazy though. Like you have every cancer in the book. Only good thing is its progress seems incredibly slow. The oncologist is freaked out that you aren't dead already."

"Cancer." My sigh was louder than I intended. "Well, I guess that explains everything. How long was I out?"

"A week. Lots of stuff happened since then." Jack interjected. "We found two more of the things and took them out. Both attacked when we cornered them. Ron barely made it. He's down in the ICU recovering from broken bones and a punctured lung. Those things are strong and fast. That one you found on the street, we were lucky there. The ones we found together almost had both of us."

Chapter 13 Ron and Jack

With me at the hospital, Ron and Jack had gone back to the grind of investigation. They went back through the names on the occult webpage and began comparing them to police records for murder investigations and missing persons online. Within a few hours they had determined that two more of those listed had died under unusual circumstances. With the two known victims and Vilma himself identified, this left three that might be alive and well.

After some checking, it turned out that all three were alive and living in various parts of the country. After contacting each, they learned that they had all been approached online at the main forum of the site to potentially join the Familia Aranea cult.

They'd agreed online and set up a kind of forum for interacting with each other. These three had become worried as they learned details of the cult's mandate. They admitted that the cultists had specifically talked about physical possession by these otherworldly pseudo-spiders.

They'd been attracted to the idea of extended life expectation and there was the promise of powers that normal humans could not attain.

This led Jack to start looking into areas of the alternate religion site that I'd ignored. After several hours new information about Vilma had surfaced. This new information was less than six months old. In the forum they discovered several messages posted by a 'SandyVol'. The connection was too obvious. Near the end of the thread was contact information for the leader of a cult called Kult der Spinnen.

The fact that the cult leader was playing on the idea of mysticism based on a spider meant that he was obviously attempting to use terms that humans could understand. The general appearance of the creature was not unlike a spider.

Ron found that the contact information was on a hosted website and with the help of a federal warrant he was able to get the hosting service to release billing information on the e-mail service. This gave him an address near Santa Fe, New Mexico. He was also rewarded with an actual name. Manuel Soussol lived out of the way area north of Glorieta.

As Jack drove, Ron continued to review the case file. Recently he'd added several documents to the manila folder he'd shown me. These included lab reports and speculative information I'd provided.

They arrived at the address provided near mid-day. The rambling mission style home was typical of the area. An outer wall with curved contours surrounded the yard. A tall arched entry was barred by wrought iron gates bent in unique shapes. The house itself had vigas jutting out from below the parapet. Scuppers and downspouts traced their way from the roof level to the ground at each corner. Though the wood of the door appeared old and distressed under the heavy clear finish, it was probably relatively new. At the center of the door about two thirds of the way up was a large iron ring knocker.

Ron grasped the ring and wrapped three times. After a moment, the sound of someone walking on hard flooring was heard. The door opened a crack. The face of an aged Hispanic woman peered out from behind the heavy frame.

"Ma'am, I'm Ron Hatch and this is Jack McMinn. We'd like to speak to Mr. Vilma." Ron flashed his FBI ID and badge.

A nervous look crossed her face. "He isn't here right now." She insisted.

"Do you know where he has gone and when he'll be back?" Ron continued to press for information.

"He sometimes is gone for weeks." She said. If it's important I could give you his phone number."

"Thank you. That will be helpful." Ron wasn't ready to let her go yet. "Do you know where he goes when he travels?"

"He went to a meeting in Albuquerque." She offered. "I have the itinerary if you would like."

"Yes we would. Thank you."

She opened the door a little and waived them in. then she left them standing in the foyer and wandered into a room off to the left. After a minute she returned with several sheets of printed paper from a booking site which had a hotel and meeting room reserved for several days.

The investigators asked a few more questions but she was either not talking or she didn't know much more. She seemed to genuinely be telling the truth as she insisted at each question that she didn't know the answer.

They returned to Albuquerque knowing Vilma had at least one more day of meetings. This gave them time to set up a stakeout and just watch his comings and goings for the day. Ron figured they'd move in just before he headed north.

He spent a great deal of time in business meetings. It seemed he was involved in real estate. He'd earned a reputation of being very informed about the state of the financials involved in property development.

He was currently lecturing on leveraging buyouts for large scale commercial property. It explained the expensive home in Glorietta as well as his other properties.

During the stake out, they received information on his various accounts indicating that he was worth a considerable amount. It seemed at odds with the idea that he could be an otherworldly parasite. Jack made the joke that he was possibly a real estate parasite as well as a brain parasite. Ron didn't seem amused.

At the end of the first day they recognized the Sandoval woman when she walked across the hotel lobby to meet up with Vilma. A man was tagging along. He was in his early forties and dressed well. His nervous disposition indicated he was uncomfortable with whatever was happening.

Jack and Ron saw this as the opportunity they needed. The three walked out the main entrance together. Once outside they entered a new black sedan.

Ron called for a track on the car by license number and was happy to discover that the car had GPS enabled navigation. He was rewarded with the movements of the vehicle by phone allowing them to stay well behind the car during the ensuing tail.

After about fifteen minutes of winding through the streets, the car stopped in front of a newer home in an upscale northeast area not far from where they'd found what they started to refer to as the decoy body. A call to the dispatcher gave the owner of the residence as Jonathan Perkins.

The home was a large ranch style of stucco without embellishment. A large xeriscaped yard was interrupted on each side by small lawns. The walk leading to the front door was laid from red cement hexagons bordered with red scalloped cement edging.

They waited for another twenty minutes before deciding to make contact with the suspects. Though procedure called for backup, they decided against it because of the paranormal nature of the investigation.

Ron knocked on the black six panel door.

After a short pause the door opened and the woman identified as Sandoval answered and simply said "Yes."

"I'm Agent Hatch and this is detective McMinn. We are checking into the death of a woman not far from here. May we come in?"

"I have guests right now. Could you come back later?" She answered in a calm voice.

"No, I think we'd like to talk to them as well." Ron insisted.

"OK." She opened the door a little more but not quite enough for them to enter. Then she said. "Do you have a warrant?"

"No Ma'am. This is simply an inquiry." Ron replied.

"I'm not sure then that I would like to offer you access to my home." She said.

"Ms. Sandoval, this isn't your home. Is Mr. Perkins at home so we can talk to him?"

A sudden burst of movement resulted in the door being slammed. From behind the door the sounds of running and some muffled shouts burst forth.

Jack stepped back, pulled out his firearm and kicked the door just to the side of the knob. The door splintered around the lock and swung open. Ron had his pistol in his hands pointed into the hallway as the door swung open.

Ron said "Right."

"Left" Jack responded.

They moved into the house quickly. They checked a door to the right that turned out to be a bathroom. Slowly they came to the main living area after a short hallway of six feet. The left wall continued on. The right hand wall opened into the living space. Jack set up low and knelt forward, looking into the area.

149

"Clear" he called. Then he added. "Kitchen to the right, hallway ahead."

Jack turned the corner bringing his aim up. His body angled to present the smallest target. Ron followed as Jack sidestepped to his left to get a better view into the kitchen.

Movement down the hall caught their attention. They followed quickly but not without checking the kitchen area to make sure there was no ambush waiting from them.

Slowly they moved down the hallway. Guessing the layout from having seen the outside of the house the doors on the right would be bedrooms and the door at the end of the hallway was probably the garage. Another door on the left might be another bedroom or a bath.

As they inched toward the first door Jack maintained his view down the hall as Ron reached for the doorknob with his left hand. As he started to turn the knob the door burst open in an explosion of splinters. Ron was thrown against the far wall of the hallway blocking Jack's progress forward missing him by only a few inches.

A medium build man stepped quickly through the door. He reached over with astonishing speed and slapped Ron across the back of his right hand, forcing him to drop his weapon. The man then kicked upward toward Ron's face.

Caught full in the face, Ron flipped over backward in an awkward summersault that ended in him landing on Jack.

Jack barely had a chance to get his weapon out of the way and prepare for the collision. He turned his body slightly to absorb most of the impact while still maintaining a field of fire on the assailant.

The attacker came forward, bending over Ron, reaching with both hands. Jack fired twice at his center mass. The man staggered backward a step then came forward again. Jack fired twice more. The man did not slow at all as he gripped Ron by one leg and just below his shoulder. He was hauling Ron up over his head when Jack adjusted his aim and fired twice more into the man's face. He dropped Ron and reached for Jack in the same way. Jack was unable to continue firing for fear of hitting his partner.

Jack staggered backward and managed to get to his feet before he was grabbed. Taking careful aim, he fired again.

The man stiffened. His face was bloody and broken from several gunshot wounds. The eyes, still intact, lost the luster of intelligence. He fell forward and crashed to the floor with a loud slapping sound.

Ron was staggering to his feet when Sandoval stepped from the battered doorway and grabbed his wrist and twisted. The sound of the bone snapping was overwhelmed by Ron's shriek of pain. He turned toward her and brought up his recovered gun attempting to fire.

Her other hand shot forward and knifed into his shoulder making him drop his gun again. Then she kicked him in the chest. The front kick would normally have been the kind meant to push your opponent back, similar to a shove. The confines of the hall meant that all the power was transmitted into his body without any way to backpedal. He gave a loud "humpf" then fell to the floor.

Jack stepped forward, firing his pistol at Sandoval. She dodged under the shots. As she moved forward, Jack fired again but the slide locked back indicating that the magazine was empty.

Sandoval moved in rapidly as Jack backed into the living room. As Jack backed away, he dropped his magazine and loaded another. The slide locked forward just as she launched another attack. From a forward cat stance, her round kick forced jack back farther.

As he leaned out of the way, he settled his aim and fired again. She leaned to the right as the bullet passed her without hitting the mark. Her leaning movement allowed her to reach out with her right hand and stab at Jack's gun hand.

She hit him just behind the wrist, bringing a shock of pain that almost made him drop his weapon. Her left hand then came forward and punched him in the sternum, forcing him back further.

By now he was leaning backward over the back of the couch. With a slight jump he bounced over the couch, landing in the seat with his legs in the air. Two more shots rang out, one hitting her just below the jaw line on the left side of her neck.

She jumped over the couch in a single bound, landing behind Jack.

Jack shifted his position and rolled backward as she jumped, maintaining aim if not composure. Another two shots rang out both hitting the target one in the leg and the other in the lower abdomen. Jack tumbled to the floor, one leg crashing hard on the oak coffee table.

She reached over and grabbed the leg. In a show of incredible strength, she lifted him off the floor by the leg using only one hand. Jack fired again after bringing his aim higher. This time both rounds hit her full in the face.

Her face shattered in a shower of blood and bone. She stiffened and fell where she stood, dropping Jack to the floor.

Jack staggered to his feet. He wiped the blood and gore from his face with the sleeve of his jacket. He holstered his weapon then moved over to check on Ron. Ron was awake and moving. He cradled his arm in a way that made Jack think he'd broken it. A quick check told Jack that Ron would be ok if he got medical attention quickly.

Jack called in on his two-way. He requested ambulance and a crime scene unit.

Checking the first attacker, he found the man was dead. Most of his face and head had been damaged from the close range gunshots. From the back of his head, a large spider-like thing had half emerged. Several of the shots had penetrated the creature. It seemed to be dead as well.

He moved back to check on the Sandoval woman. Her injuries were similar to those of the other attacker. The creature however seemed to still be alive and was moving slowly.

Jack stepped away disgusted by the thing moving in her head. He thought of a way to kill it. Remembering that our environment was deadly to it, he picked up a piece of broken wood from the coffee table and tried to pry it out of her head. The thing just dug in deeper. The effort was making him sick. Eventually he realized he was not going to get it out and stopped.

He fell to his knees and vomited.

In the distance he heard the sound of sirens approaching.

Chapter 14 Cancer

As I listened to Jack tell me what they'd gone endured, several thoughts went through my head. First being that destruction of these creatures could be achieved with normal weapons. Second, what happened to the thing in Sandoval? Third was, how were we going to find the last one of these spider cult guys? He was obviously aware that we'd found him out and would be taking steps to avoid capture.

"What happened to the thing that seemed to still be alive?" I asked.

"Dead now. The M.E. cut open the head during autopsy. The thing scared the crap out of him, then died within a couple of seconds. Seems like when the underside gets exposed to the air, the thing dies. The first one was basically shot to pieces. The one in Sandoval was mostly intact. When the M.E. pulled off the skull cap the thing tried to bury itself deeper but there was no place for it to go. It shriveled up and died in seconds." Jack explained.

"That's something at least." I responded. "Am I cleared to leave the hospital?"

"I don't know. I can ask." Hector said. He stepped out of the room.

"Jack, I have to do something that might leave you guys to finish this by yourselves." Admitting that my dreams were important after everything else we'd gone through was still a bit of a stretch. I already probably seemed like an egotistical nut job to them. I didn't explain the reason or the task.

Hector came back in followed by Lucy and a doctor who looked very concerned.

The doctor asked how I felt. I told him I felt fine even though I had a low grade headache that was just painful enough to be annoying without being debilitating.

"Mr. Jenisen, you have got to understand we have no idea what is happening to you. There seems to be signs of several forms of cancer. Each alone is terminal. You seem to be managing them somehow. But I couldn't tell you how long you have. I can only say it's not very long. We could do some chemo to stall the progress a bit. I'd be able to get you a medical marijuana prescription. You could at least be comfortable that way." The doctor was at least being honest.

"No thanks." I smiled. "I have this bucket list so… when can I get out of here?"

"There's no need to keep you here. I'll start you being processed out." He said.

I was out of the hospital in less than two hours. Jack and Lucy drove me to their home and offered me lunch. Hector had to return to the lab which was just up the hill from the hospital I was being treated at.

The day was warming and though the house had air conditioning, I felt like I was too hot. I wondered if it was the feeling of having been told I was dying, or a symptom of my ailment.

The lunch was a sandwich and lemonade. It made me feel better. Very little conversation was to be had. I think they both seemed to want to leave me to my thoughts and really that's where I wanted to be as well.

I thought about all the things I'd need to do, get my will in order, pay a few bills, maybe go hang gliding? I guess it hadn't really occurred to me that I'd have a limited number of days. Maybe I just didn't think about it too much. With a limit that was undefined, how was I to know how much I might get done before the end.

If I hurried through a bucket list anything on the list would not get proper attention. I didn't think I'd enjoy the process at all anyway. So what does someone who knows he is going to die soon do with his undefined limit?

Well I have one friend that has offered friendship without any other consideration. That friend needs help and I am the only one who can help. It seems like that would be a good place to start. Grieta would be pleased that I would make the effort to help.

The challenge was I had no idea what to do. I asked if the geode was still in Jack's keeping. He said yes.

I asked if I could use it for a while. He said yes, and gave me the geode in a shoebox. He said he put it in there as it was glowing in a strange way for the last several days. The glow had faded just this morning when he'd gotten up.

I said thank you and walked back to my hotel with the box in my arm like a baby. It felt comfortable to have it. I felt as though I was holding a friend's hand as I walked along in the hot early afternoon sun.

A feeling of calm determination came over me.

There is an old Samurai idea that you must accept that in the coming battle you will die. That way you will not let fear of death stop you from doing what you must. It was a straight forward and very pragmatic ideal that somehow seemed to fit the situation.

When I got back to the hotel I called Maria and told her the news. She cried. I guess I could have been more tactful but it didn't seem to be worth the effort. After all she was strong and brave.

Then I called the family lawyer. It was he who had informed me of the death of my parents just under a year ago. That information and the subsequent financial freedom had started me on the journey that eventually will see me buried next to them.

I had him draw up papers on what to do with my things when I die. Who gets what, and how. I won't bore you with the details because it hasn't happened yet. This simple act gave me a sudden clarity about the task to come.

I decided it was time to contact Grieta and figure out what I'd need to do to fight off the mentalities that were trying, even now, to control the gateway. Our minds came into focus together as I finished the spell that allowed contact.

"I'm nearly ready to come and help." I thought.

"I'm glad". It thought back

"What will I need to do?"

"You will cross into my consciousness. Here, what you think and what you imagine is reality. You frame your own interpretation of my existence."

"I don't understand". I thought again.

"Don't worry, you will understand when you come into me". Grieta informed me.

"My mentality can be a framework but your mind must interpret what it senses. There is no analogue for experience. This gives you the ability to define the encounter. Whatever you encounter in my mentality will be understood by you as only your mind can offer the necessary environment to allow for existence within this place."

"I still don't understand but I will give it a try." I thought.

"Rest first. Be with your friends when you come. This way if something bad happens they can be close at hand to retrieve you."

"Retrieve me? I know that it's possible for me to die. I'm not worried about that."

"Dying is only one outcome. You might succeed. You might become lost. If that happens there will be nothing they can do to retrieve you unless one is willing to stand at the contact point. Then they can be as a lighthouse. You will see the way home for as long as they are near it."

"OK."

I broke off contact. The connection with Grieta was draining emotionally. I always feel drained afterword. I've been told that regular people feel something like that when they breakup with a longtime girlfriend, or maybe the feeling of getting divorced. It's like I lose the better part of myself when contact is broken.

It was nearing 10:00 pm when I'd finished. I showered and shaved. Got myself ready for bed then laid in bed thinking till my mind slipped into the black.

The dragon was there. It was gold and orange. The long sinuous body covered in scales. Heavy whiskers of black hair fanned from the snout that seemed more the face of a lion than that of a snake. The front claws were strong and sharp. From just behind the forelegs, wings that were small but shaped like the fins of a goldfish fluttered in the air around it. The rear legs were like those of a large predatory cat. The long golden tail ended in a vertical fin similar to the wings.

It looked into my eyes as it sat upon a throne of jade and onyx. Those eyes were dark and deep. As I stared into them I realized they were familiar to me. The dragon coiled on the throne as it watched me. As its coils wound in and out I saw that it held in the folds of its body a sphere that radiated blackness though the color of the sphere itself was deep blue.

This marble-like orb had at its center a pale white glow. At first it seemed to be a steady and constant light. As the moments passes I realized the glow faded in time with the beating of a heart. And the intensity of the black which radiated from it was in time to a breathing that accompanied the heartbeat.

The dragon spoke suddenly but softly in a feminine voice. "I will guard the center while you do battle with the daemons from the other world."

The dream faded quickly and I was awake.

I looked at the clock on the nightstand and found that it was nearly 7 am. I decided to get up and work out in the hotel gym for a while. After that I'd get breakfast and call Hector. It was Hector I'd need for the next part of this because I realized as I awoke that the dragon that guards the center was Min, his wife.

Chapter 15 Min

Min was born on a cool spring day. Her mother was young, being only 21. Her father was older, in his late thirties. Though uncommon, arranged marriages were still an occasional practice for traditionally-minded Chinese families.

She had no memory of her mother. Her father insisted she'd left shortly after delivering her into the world.

Her father was very traditional in his manner. He lived in a home in southern California with the entire extended family. His parents and two aunts also shared the four bedroom house. Though the home was crowded, Min was afforded the luxury of her own room. One of the bedrooms was reserved for the 4 other children and the aunts. Grandfather and grandmother had a room. Father also had a room of his own.

It was her Grandfather who saw to her education. He taught her alchemy and traditional medicine as well as the particular family tradition of defending against the creatures from the world beneath the world.

Each generation was tasked with guardianship of the gateway. Though it was no longer accessible, she was found to have the disposition of a guardian and was therefore the focus of her grandfathers' lessons.

He woke her early every morning before dawn and began her lessons with basic martial arts. In her early years he taught her the Tan Tui forms. By her early teens she was well versed in several internal styles including Tai Chi, Pauqua, and Xiangyi. As she graduated high school she completed several external forms. The most important was a small family style called the Wu Xian. This style places focus on the five elements and the five animals in relationship to five phases and colors. The basic tenant is that this style has physical effects as well as subtly woven mystical elements allowing the user a basic anti-corruption spell casting ability.

She was also instructed in special forms of writing and alchemy that would allow her to generate chi fields to aid in combating any evil creature she might encounter.

Her studies were difficult but she mastered everything her Grandfather taught her. She was also very apt at her regular class room studies. Her grades were always at the top of the class.

Other than school and the studies her grandfather offered she had no other duties to perform in the household. Because of her special situation she was afforded a great deal of respect from the rest of the family. She was, however, protected from much of regular life.

She was never allowed to date or engage in any after school activity including sports. Though she had friends in school, she was not allowed to socialize with them after school or on the weekend. Even her summer break months were dedicated to an accelerated curriculum from her grandfather.

It was clear from the beginning that her entire family loved her and doted on her, but they also protected her to the point she occasionally rebelled. The few times she stayed out after school or snuck out she felt so guilty afterword that she apologized profusely and tried very hard not to let her rebellious nature come out.

Though she lived in southern California, she was offered an academic scholarship to attend University of New Mexico. She accepted without any thought to the family simply because she felt like it would be good to get out from under the constant gaze of the family. To her surprise her family had no objections.

During the first year away she met Hector in a biology class. Though shy she took to him quickly. His gregarious nature and optimistic outlook made her feel comfortable and free.

They'd dated for more than a year before they became intimate. Hector patiently waited for her to be ready and she grew to love him more and more for his loving and giving nature.

She was highly amused when he acted like a tough guy. She'd tried to teach him some of the family martial arts but he hadn't the patience for it.

Her family came for the graduation. They met Hector for the first time. Again she was surprised when they offered no resistance to her marrying him. They were married less than six months later at a ceremony during the Balloon Fiesta.

Since then she and Hector had led a pretty ordinary life. She maintained a martial arts school in a strip mall south of the university. Her students occasionally competed and always did very well at the tournaments.

I wondered at the revelations I'd had lately. With everything happening, the last thing I wanted to do was worry about myself. It did seem as though everything that had happened to me over the last few months was brought on by my suddenly selfish desire to get away from being responsible.

I'd fought against having my family place so much responsibility on me. Even though I did follow the rules and perform as expected, I also pushed the boundaries quite a bit. There are times when I wonder if my father knew about my rebellions, if he was aware of my comic book collection. I spend a great deal of time day dreaming as well. Those were some of the ways I expressed my dissatisfaction.

By the time I'd headed to college the expression was a more pertinent and formalized decision to stay in the city. Which somehow lead to my dissatisfaction with my life in general. I harbored resentment for my parents for a long time for not giving me a normal life. After a while I realized, they were not the cause of my personal issues with my life. They had tried to offer me what they thought was best and in the end I recognized how much they loved me. By then it was really too late to tell them so. I doubt that my father would have approved of an open display of affection. I often thought that my mother might actually break down and cry in happiness if I told her I understood and that I loved her. Such are my fantasies.

Hector agreed to meet me. After consulting with Jack we decided to attempt the crossing at Jack and Lucy's home. We met in the early afternoon. Jack and Lucy offered some snacks and coffee.

Hector and Min seemed excited in a strange way. I decided to explain the situation as I'd come to understand it before we started the experiment.

We sat there in the living room. The Geode was sitting in the center of the oak coffee table. Hector and I sat in two chairs from the dining room. Min sat in the armchair. Jack and Lucy were on the couch.

"The gate is a contact plane between our world and other worlds. Some of these other worlds are populated with beings which are trying to take over our world. They are, by our standards, alien and evil. I can't think of any other way to say it. What I've seen so far is that they take over the body and mind of people and force them to do their bidding. They can reanimate dead bodies for a time to achieve small gains in our world. From what I've read they can even take over the minds of animals and reshape them somewhat to forms that are more suitable for their needs. There are a few creatures that can actually exist in our world. These are very powerful. The brain spiders and a few others can exist for very small amount of time outside the host. From what Jack described it's a very narrow timeframe for them."

"There are even a few creatures that are very powerful that can exist in our world without hosts. I suspect that they are still vulnerable to various spells and devises such as the dagger I described earlier that we used to destroy the first creature I encountered and maybe even simple weapons like guns and such."

"My point is, the beings use mental possessions as their primary form of attacking our world. Somehow they seem to have developed a way of potentially controlling the mentality that is the rift. I call it Grieta. Min refers to it simply as The Center. Whatever we call it, Grieta has finally decided to take a side. In the past, The Center simply observed and allowed passage as long as it wasn't affected by the long standing activities between the invaders and us."

"There have been recent developments which have caused the rift to take action on our behalf. Somewhere a gate was violently opened causing distress to Grietas' mind. This seemed to have been caused by the other half of the geode which forms a kind of parallel gateway with the one we now possess. The rift was weakened enough by this action for the evil to begin the process of possessing the mentality of the rift."

"Interestingly, Grieta tells me the half of geode we possess was not used recently, making me wonder if the cult Familia Aranea may have only recently come into possession of this half."

"If the rift is taken over... well it won't be good for us. I will try to enter the rift and do battle with whatever evil has invaded it. I asked Min to come because she is a Rift Guardian, trained to do battle with and protect our world from anything that might come across and I'm confident she can pull me out if things don't go as planned."

"Pull you out?" Jack asked.

"Look, this is new for me. All I know is what Grieta told me. It will be dangerous and I need someone here in case it gets bad to pull me out. It will require that she hold onto something of mine. To act as an anchor." I handed her the jeweled dagger. "This weapon was used to destroy the first creature I fought. Since then I've been given charge of it by the Drakson family. I think it will serve well as an anchor."

"I know what you need." Min told us. "This will be my anchor for you. It will act as a focus to keep the gate open while you are in the other world. Also I must be ready if anything tries to cross into our world." Min placed it reverently on the coffee table next to the Geode.

"OK." I said. "Anybody got any ideas?"

"What do we know about it?" Hector asked. "I mean I'm just a biologist."

"I don't know. I was just…"

"Let's get started." I finally said.

I leaned forward toward the Geode. I felt the very nearness of the entity that is Grieta in the stone and crystal.

I uttered the spell of contact and waited a moment then uttered it again.

The feeling of contact came rapidly. My mind was in connection to the rift and I could feel the voice of Grieta in my thoughts. "Come into me." it said.

Just then I felt a touch on my shoulder. Hector had leaned in and just brushed me with his hand as I let my mind move into Grietas' mind.

The feeling was calm and warm. I can only describe it as something like the euphoria from drinking without the loss of control. I felt like I could do anything.

I heard, felt Grieta tell me. "You have brought another."

"I'm sorry." I heard Hector say.

My vision was clouded for a moment with mist. Then a world came to life. I heard the sounds of birds and saw this deep cleft in the rocks ahead of me. Looking down I could see that I stood on an outcropping of rock high in the mountains. Small brown grasses and stunted trees surrounded me.

There next to me stood Hector. He was wearing the clothes I'd seen him in when we first met. The red flannel shirt was again buttoned at the top. The bandanna covered his eyebrows and partially obscured his eyes. He had a puzzled look on his face. "What happened?"

"You came into me with Chris." Grieta told us. "You must now complete the task with him. He was the guiding mind so you will experience the world here in my mentality as he projects it."

"I don't understand." I said.

"My consciousness has no form. No buildings or pathways. My mind is not a construct of physical things. It is a place of thoughts. Since my mind is far beyond anything you can experience, you must experience it by how your mind interprets, and therefore projects, events. In a real way you will define your experience here."

"But you said it would be Chris that guides what happens. Why?" Hector asked.

"He said the spell. And he is my friend."

Hector seemed satisfied with that answer. "OK, what now?"

"Yes," I added. "What now."

"You must search within my consciousness for the invading mentalities and destroy them."

"I'm sorry, I guess, I don't know how to do that." I admitted.

"Begin my looking for something that is out of place. Then go to it." Grieta said.

I scanned the scene for anything that didn't seem to fit. What would it look like? What was I looking for? No answer came to my mind. The sky was deep grey covered in slow moving storm clouds. Near me from my left to right a trail wound downward to the depth of the chasm.

Scant vegetation dotted the landscape. The rock was striated and layered. It seemed to be a combination of granite and sandstone mixed with the occasional layer of a darker rock.

I could not really see the bottom of the chasm. A fine light grey mist shrouded the depths and trailed menacingly upward between the rocky crags.

Across from us, in the distance, I could make out the other side of the canyon. It was similar in geology to our side with the exception being that I could not make out any vegetation.

About half way up on the opposite slope I saw a faint light. Small and yellow, it wavered slightly as though it was from a torch. I could see a path leading to it from below. I squinted my eyes and made out the path climbing up from the light. It was very geometric in design and seemed very out of place. My eyes were drawn to several dark figures moving around near the light.

That must be the thing we were meant to deal with. The path downward seemed our only possibility for getting across so I started down.

Hector walked along side me in silence. After a few minutes I realized he looked at me with a quizzical look every time he glanced in my direction.

"What?" I asked.

"Take a look homey." He nodded at me.

I looked down at my clothes and saw that I was garbed in the same clothing that the Draksons wore. Black slacks and jacket lined and traced all over with satin threaded writing from a dozen lost languages. The white linen dress shirt was similar except the threads making the writing were of white satin.

I felt a small bit of pressure then at my hip and opened the jacket to discover the cause. There in a small leather sheath was a short sword. I recognized it as the one that Kayle used against the creature.

I smiled at the thought that I had assumed these clothes. Somewhere in my subconscious mind I had made a deep connection to the Drakson family. I knew now that I'd felt more for them than I had for anyone in my somewhat lonely life. To feel this way now seemed to be an epiphany of sorts.

"All you got is a sword?" Hector asked. "I got this." He reached behind him and withdrew a large chromed pistol. It seemed almost too large for his hand. He smiled then tucked it into the back of his khakis.

I smiled back and continued my descent.

After a few minutes I said. "I think both might become useful."

The path downward was rocky. Occasionally we were forced to climb over large boulders or piles of rock. A few times this mountaineering led to one or the other of us slipping and dislodging rocks that fell into the chasm between us and our objective.

The layer of mist below seemed rolled in even waves as though it corresponded to the rhythm of someone breathing. The trail finally dipped into it. Once in the mist I could tell that the landscape had changed around us. It became less rough. The path below our feet was smooth. Another few steps and we were below the layer.

The mist above us rolled as though tossed by an unfelt wind. The environment no longer had any features. The path was simply a slightly different colored band of subdued grey that wound downward. Perspective had somehow shifted so that it seemed we sped along the trail to the bottom in only a few moments.

At the bottom was a river. The dark grey featureless surface flowed slowly from left to right. We wandered up the bank looking for a way to cross. The bank of the river was as featureless as the water that flowed. The abrupt straight edge between the river and the shore was only defined by the fact that the river moved and the shore did not.

There seemed to be no bridge or ford to give us access to the other side. Finally I decided to simply swim across. I stepped into the water and found that it was not very deep at the edge. I could feel the flow around my ankle but the flow only came up to my mid calf.

My second step was no deeper. As I moved my first foot forward I found that the fluid was thicker than water. It took much more effort to push my feet through the river than it would for normal water.

A soft voice informed us. "This is my center, where all worlds meet. To cross from any portal to another you will always cross the center."

"Is this like your mind?" Hector asked.

"A good analogy. Not entirely accurate. Nothing here is separate from my consciousness. This is my center from where flows the streams of my thoughts. This is more closely identified as my heart."

I smiled and thought of us crossing into the heart of Grieta. The crossing seemed difficult but soon we were stepping out onto the smooth shore. I saw to the left the path that would lead us upward to the enemy.

Hector and I began our climb and were soon above the mist.

The features of grey boulders and cliff faces returned. Again we were faced with rough climbing. Sometimes the path was no more than a few inches of stone projected out above the emptiness.

"What happens if we fall?" I asked.

"The same as if you fall in your world. You might die." Grieta informed me.

This made me hug the cliff face tighter and grip each bit of rock that served as a hand and foot hold. I eased my pace somewhat trying to be as safe as possible. In doing so the way seemed to be even more difficult as though my slowing affected a change in the fabric of the place. Perhaps haste was necessary and this was my subconscious mind alerting me to the fact. Perhaps it was Grieta telling me to hurry.

I picked up the pace again and the way became somewhat easier. Still there were obstacles that barred the way but we made it through without injury.

At last we came upon a place where we could see the enemy. Hiding behind a boulder we spied upon their efforts.

There were five creatures. Each shaped loosely like a man. They were tall and thin with deep chests. The long legs had extra joints that bent at an odd backward angle. The long six fingered hands sported wicked looking claws. The heads were triangular. The pointed bottoms and wide tops were slightly curved, creating a domed effect. There were no features in the faces. No noses mouths or eyes to disrupt the dark grey visage.

Their legs were anchored in the rock but moving with it, making ripples of stone where they stepped. With each step the rock became organized and reformed to exacting geometry. The angles were disturbing though. It was as though some weird non-Euclidian math had formed the basis of the design.

Now I had to decide what action to take. It seemed as though the damage they were doing was being done by their feet, if I could call them feet. Maybe if I knocked them off their feet. I wondered if I could find a way to keep them from reattaching and doing more damage.

As these plans were forming in my mind Hector suddenly jumped up from behind the rock where we had hidden, and began firing his pistol. The loud crack of each shot rang across the canyon loudly, leaving a ringing in my ears.

Without hesitating I ran to follow him.

His first few shots punched into the nearest of the creatures. As they passed into it, the thing resolved into nothingness, slowly fading to intangibility.

That solved the problem of how to destroy them. I raced to the nearest one and swung the short sword at its neck. It interjected its forearms and swung at me with the opposite arm. It caught me in the chest. This produced a sharp pain from its claws raking into me. I twisted my body to avoid as much of the attack as I could and leaned into a jab with the tip of my weapon.

I caught it under a slight bulge in its chest area that maybe coincided with the sternum. My blade passed completely though with a small amount of resistance.

As I pulled the blade free the thing also dissolved from view leaving a wisp of windblown dust.

Hector had fired several more shots, killing two more of the things. Now his pistol was empty. He patted his pockets looking for another magazine. While distracted, the last of the creatures had approached him from behind.

As I shouted at Hector that the thing was behind him, I scrambled forward. Time seemed to slow for me as Hector turned to look. I could see the expression of surprise and fear. I realized I would not reach the thing in time and threw my sword to try to at least distract it.

The sword flew straight and true. The point entered the creature's body where the neck met the shoulder. It penetrated several inches. The creature turned toward me and pawed at the blade sticking out from its neck.

Hector had fully turned and changed his hold on the gun. Using it like a hammer he smashed the thing in the head. Then he grabbed the handle of the sword and pulled it free. A gout of sparkling dust burst forth from the wound. The creature sank to its knees and fell over. Then it began to dissolve into dust.

Hector thanked me and handed me the blade. He found that he was out of ammunition for the pistol and tossed it aside. "We got them right? No need for this anymore."

"I think so. Now about this path. Grieta, do we need to do something about it?" I asked.

Grieta answered. "It is their way into my mind. It is the scar of them violating my mind, forcing their will upon me. It is painful and shameful. I have no control of the place they have touched. It must be reshaped or they will still have access. Though they've stopped building it, they are pressing for control even now."

What would we be able to do that might return this path to its original form? I thought about the idea of maybe blasting it with a spell or an avalanche.

As I was detailing these and other potential ways of dealing with the problem Grieta answered again in a soft almost alluring voice. "You can join with my memory and recreate the path as you interpret it from my mind."

"How?"

"You have a spell that will allow you to focus on residual memories. This place is my mind. Once you find the memory, your mind will interpret it. Then you can walk the path and mentally replace the design with the original image. That image is your interpretation of my memories. It is good that you brought Hector. He can protect you while you are engaged. The Master might try again to access my mind."

"OK, I'll try. Give me a moment."

The place was somewhat disconcerting and although I realized that my focusing chant was effective. What I see are things that have past from the perspective of the person who expressed the most emotional stresses. I had a connection with a non-human memory once and it was very difficult. I took a few moments to ready myself for the task.

I handed Hector the sword. I closed my eyes. I began the chant. "Upon the point of a needles eye your eye must focused be. Through the eye of a needle's point, the truth is what you'll see."

I felt a slight rush as my mind was brought into full focus. There within my mind I found its mind. I struggled for a few minutes as images and sounds and smells and the feeling of other senses I couldn't begin to understand flooded through me. As I focused only on the visual cues, the others dropped away. History from a thousand worlds played in my sight. I found the ones for our world and let them run through me rapidly. Then I tried to focus on the local memories. I caught the smell of a wildflower.

The memory was without form. I felt it and I slipped into it and tried to see it with my mind's eye. In a few more moments it came into focus and I played back from where I was through to when it started.

There Hector and I stood talking to Grieta in reverse. Then a backward battle played where each of the creatures came to life before our weapons did their work, before we came upon the scene here, before they came.

I looked at the geometric pattern and compared it with the roughly shaped natural rock that should have been there, the rock that was there in my memory, in Grieta's memory. Over the millennium and through the ages, slowly surely Grieta observed. In observing, Grieta became aware. In awareness Grieta became cognizant of self. Once aware of self, she began to understand her loneliness.

That rock should be there, and it was. This part should not be so flat. These cracks in the stone are not at perfect angles, the edges are rougher. This part slopes more. Here is a ledge that narrows and winds in and around an outcropping that is of a darker stone.

She played with the boundaries of her universe. She longed to express, but had no way of expressing, her feeling of isolation. In a moment that was a century and an infinite time span, she tore open her mind to seek other consciousness to have companionship. That was how the gateways were created.

From these she could explore and see life expand and take root on a million worlds. As she looked, so then life began. Some life was dark and sinister, some life was innocent and without stain.

Then I took a step, knowing that this small slice had been repaired. After another revision of the rock I took another step. Onward I went one step at a time.

She loved to look in on the innocent places, where the creatures knew no sorrow or pain. Here and there creatures of all forms lived in simple cycles of life. Sometimes they died as was their nature. Each form lived to fulfill its place in the cycle of life.

Occasionally I had to backtrack as I saw the natural form from a different angle. Each step was a timeless effort in rebuilding, or in this case unbuilding the damage that had been done. I cannot say how long it took. It seemed to me to be an eternity. Another step was taken, and those pebbles scattered like so. There above the horizontal crack should be striation of soft colors. Red, brown, grey, and blackish rock all work together to form the non-pattern of Grieta.

More steps, each an effort of patience and will. My heart was beating faster and my breath becoming deeper. I continued anyway. For a lifetime I walked slowly. I forgot about Hector. I forgot about myself.

All my mind could latch on to were the shapes that should have been replacing the forms that couldn't be. My entire existence became the rebuilding of Grieta. Each stone was a memory, each color a thought, each crack a long forgotten idea.

Grieta slowly began to realize what it had lost, how it should think and be, and that it could act. There in the last moments of my walking step by step up the precarious trail along the cliff face that was its memory, I came to realize what Greta was. Grieta was that spark that forms the beginning.

She'd made contact with creatures in a few worlds and gave them help in small ways. Each of these beings seemed to view her as a sort of deity. Generally, they attempted to contact her for some purpose which seemed to have a connection with the death of their physical form. A few of the cultures even used the contact points as a way of disposing of the body. After a time she realized that it was meant as a sort of offering and it had something to do with an emotional need.

She found that she could connect with creatures while they slept. She could see the dreams they were having. Later she found she could interact with them in their dreams. A few creatures were very capable and could control their dreams, giving her a way to contact them without having proximity to a gate itself.

Perhaps she should understand emotions better. If she could grasp these concepts she could communicate better with these creatures and she was curious about them. As she observed creatures from different worlds, she began to understand the basic motivations of emotion and religion.

These things were still not fully understandable since she had no fear of death. No sense of being alone. She found that she began to feel the emotion of affection for some creatures which seemed to have affection for her.

Her mind reached out and found one mind that she might exchange thoughts with. This mind felt the power of her thoughts and realized its own desire for power. It found ways to cross the rifts of her mind and enter other worlds. To control them it sent its minions. These dark evil twisted forms corrupted all they touched.

She was ashamed. She had let them in to devour the worlds of innocence. On a few worlds the evil corruption began to change the creatures, to reshape them to its will. Some fought against the rising tide of darkness and for a time, slowed its progress. She warned them. She tried to help them. The corruption was already beginning to have an effect on her. With each connection between worlds, corruption had an easier path. Each mind or physical form that passed through her, forced open her mentality to more corruption.

I saw a small bit or dark stone that seemed more a stain than anything else. It was the memory of her realizing the difference between innocence and evil. It was when she decided to try to have an effect on the evil creatures as they passed her consciousness into other worlds. She found she could slow them by placing obstacles in the way. She couldn't stop them but she could make it more difficult to pass through her.

She began to understand the motivations of the evil creatures that occasionally used her as an access point to other worlds. She decided to warn the other worlds about them if she could. Some took the warning as a sign that she was helping the evil creatures. These creatures she ignored. If they couldn't understand the warning then they would have no way to prepare for the evil. Therefore they would eventually be destroyed by it.

The Drakson family was one group that saw her as evil and she responded by ignoring their attempts at contact.

Then a contact was made from someone with an open mind. He had the spirit of desire to learn, a passion and curiosity for knowledge that rivaled hers. He contacted her through the gate that the Draksons used which made her skeptical at first. She reached to him in a dream and found his mind full of imaginative and confusing thoughts. His mind was capable of conversing with her in dreams.

She decided to trust him. When he asked a favor she tried to help him. She realized his motives were not harmful to her so she decided to continue to contact him occasionally.

The last small landing that formed an open area near the top of the high cliff face was finally returned to the image I held in my mind. It was the memory of the first time she felt alone. It was sad and grey and small pebbles of loneliness scattered about the uneven surface of the long centuries.

I came to a halt at the peak of the mountain that formed the boundary on the other side of the pass. Ahead of me I could see the angled tear in space that represented the other open gate. Hector and I stood side by side ready to cross over into it.

"How to you feel?" I asked Grieta.

"I am repaired. You have lifted the evil influence from my consciousness. Thank you."

"We should go back to the other side now." Hector said.

"There is no need. This passage is the same one you came in from." She offered.

"But we crossed that valley?" Hector insisted.

"I know you cannot understand. It is simply that each contact point is the same point in time and space within my mentality. That one point leads to all the other possible points outside of my consciousness."

"So we can go home through this rift?" I asked.

"Yes. However, the contact point on the other side was split into two parts. I see each simultaneously. You will either go home or be transported through the other gate. Either way you will be back in your world.

"So what, 50/50 chance? Let's go Vato." Hector slapped my back and strode forward.

"Thank you Grieta." I smiled.

"Thank you Chris." Grieta replied.

I followed Hector through the rift. As I passes into our world the feeling of loss came over me again.

This time it was so intense I nearly stumbled as I stepped onto a carpeted floor.

Chapter 17 Confrontation

I took a deep breath and sighed in discomfort. I had reveled in the feeling of connection to the gate. Only now that the connection was absent, I felt a real physical loss. I opened my eyes, wondering why Hector was tapping my shoulder.

We stood in a living room. It was not the living room of Jack and Lucy. This room was larger. A high ceiling was pitched toward the landing at the top of a long staircase that wound along the left hand wall. A white deep pile carpet cushioned our feet. The sunken area in the center was bordered by overstuffed custom black leather seating. The off white walls held the occasional piece of expensive art. To our backs, a double door at the other side of a deep entry foyer. A white oak coffee table with smoked glass insert held only one object, the other half of the geode.

As I reached to pick it up, a deep voice that held a strange accent told me. "That, isn't yours."

I looked up and saw what, at first, I took to be a man. The bright glow of corruption surrounded him. Again the brilliance of it indicated that this was a living creature carrying the seed of darkness. I found that I could focus enough to avoid the discomfort I'd felt before.

He was wearing a dark grey three piece suit. His tie was a thin red slash on the white shirt. He had a slightly oversized, oddly asymmetrical head from which wisps of long silver brown hair interrupted the otherwise pasty skin. Deep set dark eyes peered out from a heavy brow. The horizontal gash that was his mouth was lipless and it twitched as he spoke. "You are not wanted here. Please leave." His ragged voice sent a shiver down my back.

A feeling of dread came upon me as I gazed up at him. I sensed that this creature was not human in any way. The form was a parody of humanity.

"Sorry, I think that this needs to be protected." I picked up the stone.

He looked at me sideways for a moment then began to explain. "That stone represents something you cannot begin to fathom. I see a small amount of our life force flows in you. You do not accept it however. You try to challenge the inevitable outcome. We will prevail." His smile looked almost too human. The dark side of humanity and the evil from the other world was expressed in one evil smirk.

"You see, you cannot win against this time less evil. I myself was chosen to be a host over 400 years ago. I have become eternal and the creature that is in symbiosis with me is older even than that. Time is on our side you see. That is why you cannot win."

"We will try." Hector smiled the smile of the innocent as he responded.

The man leapt over the rail, and landed a few feet in front of me. He punched me in the center of the chest and I staggered backward. The force of the blow was tremendous and I lost my breath for a moment.

Hector backed up a couple of steps in surprise and bumped into the wall behind him. The man moved with amazing quickness and punched at Hector's face. He missed as Hector ducked low and punched the man in the midsection. The blow didn't seem to affect him. The thing then reached for Hector with both hands.

I was behind him as he moved to attack Hector and saw why his head was deformed. The upper rear portion of skin was stretched taught. Under the skin, it appeared as though fingers interlocked over a seam that ran from the center of the cranium on top, and slightly offset, to just above the base of the skull. This stretching made me think of a zipper up the back of his head.

I felt as though this might be a weakness and resolved to attack him there. I drove a round kick that caught the creature near the seam. Its head was harder than it looked. I caught it with the ball of my foot, but I didn't seem to do any damage.

The thing abandoned his attack on Hector and leaned forward as it threw a sidekick into my chest. I was thrown backward and over the couch by the force of the kick. I landed unceremoniously on my back, with my legs sprawled in the air.

Hector took advantage of the distraction caused by my failed attack and drove a haymaker up into its jaw. As the thing's head snapped back, I heard the loud crack of bones breaking and realized that Hector had not only done the creature serious damage, he had probably broken several bones in his hand.

I scrambled to my feet to again engage the enemy. I wrapped my arms around its neck in a choke-out, assuming that it would need air like any other human.

As I pressed into the hold I jumped and wrapped my legs around it for a traditional rear mount. My weight didn't seem to affect it at all so I leaned backward and pulled on my choke-out even harder. This spilled us backward onto the floor.

Suddenly something under my hand on the back of his head moved in an unnatural way. The skin stretched and I felt a movement of boney protrusions from under its skin.

The upper back of its head opened wide revealing what looked to be a curled up spider. The legs were supporting the skin as though it had held it closed like a zipper. Now as they widened I could see several small black dots that could have been eyes. Between the two rows of eyes a large jagged mouth opened. Rows of needle sharp teeth dripped with a thick slime.

I let go of my hold and tried to scramble back from the thing. The head bent backward at an odd angle, moving closer as I desperately sought to get away.

Then it shifted its arms around toward me by rotating the sockets past the normal stopping points. It reached for me. The upside down hands gripped the front of my shirt and started to draw me closer to the deadly thing now jutting partially from its head.

Holding his damaged hand close to his chest, Hector had grabbed the brass poker from the fireplace set and began smashing repeatedly at the monster nestled in the skull. Glittery gore splattered me as it loosened its grip.

After a moment, a loud sigh passed from the human mouth. Shortly after that a rustling of legs and the slacking of grip told me the thing was no longer a threat.

I pulled away quickly and stood next to Hector. My arm automatically went around his shoulder to comfort his unabashed sobbing.

"I think we got it." I said after a few minutes of patient expression.

"Th…This is wh…what you do?" he said, sobs still caused his words to stutter and his shoulders to bounce.

"Yeah, it's a bad job. I know. I should have a better insurance policy." I joked. He looked over at me and smiled. Then he patted me in the chest with his good hand. "Where the heck are we?" he asked.

I opened the map app and was rewarded with our location. I pulled my new mobile phone from my pocket and tapped it on. "Crap." I said. "I'm home."

We were in an upscale neighborhood of the relatively small city I'd grown up in. The population of less than 10,000 meant that though the town offered several of the amenities of a larger city, it also offered relative security. The fact that this was my hometown made me begin to wonder about my own upbringing.

I staggered into the kitchen and washed the slime from my face and hands. Hector did the same. Then he straightened his shirt and said. "We done here?" I nodded as I tossed the geode in the air.

"Bonus. Now we have the other half of the geode." I smiled. Hector nodded in response.

We called home. Min answered. We told her what had happened. She informed us of a problem on their end but said everything was ok. The way she said it I felt as though she was hiding something but I didn't press the issue. I informed her I was taking Hector to the hospital, for what looked like a broken wrist. She asked us to be careful.

Chapter 18 Desert Heat

Min had prepared herself as Hector and I stepped through the tear in space that hung above the geode. She felt contact with the gate's intelligence but held herself back from the act of moving through the rift. Within seconds, the rift began to glow brighter. It appeared to be a dark gash hanging in the air with a visible aura of white light surrounding it.

The aura began to fluctuate. Min stepped closer and assumed a martial arts cat stance. Her hands were open palms placed above and below in the classic form. She muttered a small spell in Cantonese just as a wave if energy exploded from the rift.

Air was displaced outward fast enough to knock everyone backward except Min. The furniture was thrown away from the center of the blast as well. The coffee table was reduced to splinters of wood.

The rift had disappeared and in its place stood a creature from the other world.

Bipedal and tall, it was roughly shaped like a man. A long toothy snout covered with gray scraggly hair jutted from the face. Tall pointed ears touched the ceiling. Its frame was sparsely covered with the same hair. The long arms and legs were heavily muscled but jointed in odd places and angles. It effused an evil that filled the home with dread.

The creature looked left then right. It turned its whole upper body as it did so, in an almost comical manner.

A loud snarl escaped as it found Min standing motionless in its view. It took a step forward on its ungainly oversized paws. Min uttered a small spell of protection then shifted back to a sideways bow stance. It attacked with its right hand in a long but amazingly fast swipe.

Min expertly dodged to the side and returned a right knife hand to the back of the passing arm. She shifted then and alternated left and right with punches to its rear midsection as she passed behind it.

It turned opposite to her direction of motion and swiped again with its arm. The blow partially caught her in the shoulder. She swept her right foot backward and away as it aimed another swipe at her face.

For a moment, the creature stopped and regarded her with its deep-set yellow eyes. A smile twisted its mouth into a grimace of joy.

"You will be fun to kill." It said in a gravelly voice.

"I will not be killed." She said in return. "I will send you back to where you came from."

"With that?" It indicated the geode. "I don't think it will work for you. You are the dragon, not the traveler."

"I am your death." She said as she shifted again into a forward stance and sent a flurry of punches and kicks at it.

It began to move in a more measured way. Now each foot was placed in an unknown pattern. Each movement of the hands was orchestrated. It jabbed with its version of a knife hand and Min slipped away by twisting her body and drove a punch into its armpit, prompting a low howl.

Then it punched at her stomach with a left that was incredibly fast. She took the blow with tightened muscles but was forced back one step.

It followed the punch quickly with a sweep from its left leg. Min dove over this and rolled to a one-legged kneeling position with both hands back to her starting double knife.

It advanced as she stood her ground. This time it attacked by attempting to grab her. She slipped to the side again but as she did, she realized it was a feint. It pulled back with the right hand as she passed under its outstretched arms. This rammed its elbow joint into the back of her head.

Again she rolled forward. This time she came all the way to her feet and kicked backward at the thing as it tried to follow up on its successful ruse.

The kick hammered into it where a human groin would have been. Though it caused the creature pain it didn't have the intended effect. It did back warily away a few steps.

Min began to devise a plan and the fight continued to resolve into a hit occasionally landed by either combatant. She began to measure the length of its steps as it moved about the floor. She watched as it moved to try to determine its range of motion and relative skill.

Finally she felt she had the right opportunity and allowed the creature to get a grasp with its clawed right hand. She reached up from below with each hand and grasped its arm just behind what would pass for a wrist. Her thumbs were on the upper wrist and fingers below.

The claws were beginning to sink into her shoulder as she suddenly dropped straight to the floor. She held on with all her strength. She was rewarded with the sound of tearing flesh. A loud pop indicated that one of its joints had separated. The monster staggered forward as she suddenly shot back up into a forward bow stance, hammering both palms into its lower jaw from below. This maneuver resulted in another loud crack indicating she'd broken bones in either the face or the jaw itself.

Again she moved quickly to harry her opponent. A series of kicks with the left foot starting at the knee and working rapidly up toward the damaged face caused it to convulse at each impact.

Finally, she spun in place and shot a knife hand forward into its neck. The fingers crushed something vital in its neck and it fell over rolling in agony.

She took a moment to look around the destroyed room. Jack was lying in a heap near the kitchen table. He looked like he was still breathing as a shallow rise and fall was evident. Lucy was near the front door in the midst of the destroyed furniture. She was beginning to rise.

Min looked back at her adversary that was writhing in agony on the floor in front of her. Though it was in severe pain, it seemed to be trying to stand and fight. After several attempts, it managed to stand partially while steadying itself against the fireplace.

Min was fascinated. It seemed that as each moment passed the creature was healing itself. First the wrist seemed to straighten followed by a snapping sound which seemed to indicate that its bones had mended. The jaw which had been slack snapped shut and, a loud popping sound followed by a grinding, startled Min.

She decided to take no more time and set herself into an aggressive stance ready to finish the thing off.

Its alarming gurgle of a voice seemed almost joyful as it chose that moment to speak again.

"I'm not that easy to destroy. I could not exist in your world if it was that easy. I've felt your power. Now it is time for you to witness mine."

A low growl came from its snarling mouth. Its arms stretched wide and seemed to elongate. Its snout pulled back into a short muzzle. The legs twisted into a new, more human, form. In only a few seconds it had transformed into a more simian shape with smaller ears at the side of its head.

Min attacked again, throwing punches to the face hoping to catch it off guard while it was still changing. Each blow struck true but seemed to have no real effect. Min's hands were aching from the impacts.

Seeing the effort as wasted she reached under its left arm and swung her body around quickly while rotating her hip into the creature. The creature flipped over Min, scraped its legs across the ceiling, and landed heavily on its back. The combined force was enough to cause it to let out a deep gasp. While it was on the floor Min dropped an ax kick into its sternum, hoping to capitalize on the damage she'd done. Again she was rewarded as the sound of crunching bone was followed by a rough sigh from it.

It punched upward at her but she stepped back to avoid the blow. Then it tried to regain its footing again.

Not waiting for a repeat of its healing and changing, she threw her fury into several punch kick combinations that kept it pinned against the wall.

She was starting to wear down due to the injuries and blood was starting to flow steadily from her shoulder. She knew she couldn't keep it up for long. She was afraid to disengage as it might have given the creature time to counter attack.

Lucy had found a hiding place behind the kitchen bar where she shuddered at the sounds of the battle.

Jack had finally regained consciousness. He staggered to his feet just as Min was starting to flag. He looked around and spotted the dagger that I'd left as an anchor, on the floor nearby. He stumbled to claim it.

Min missed a kick that left her off balance. She slipped backward as the creature pushed her away.

She desperately tried to keep her footing but the debris from the coffee table made it difficult. She landed on her injured shoulder and cried out in pain.

Jack saw the creature lean over her as she desperately tried to crawl away. Without thinking he leapt at the thing and drove the dagger deep into its chest.

The creature howled in pain and turned rapidly to face the new threat.

Jack pulled the dagger free and stabbed at it again, opening a deep wound that oozed black sparkling fluid.

As he pulled pack for another stab the thing bit deeply into his neck. His scream of pain was lost in the rending and tearing of flesh. With his last breath Jack stabbed one more time into the creature's deep set yellow eye.

It let go of the bite and slumped to the floor twitching. After a moment it stopped moving.

Jack fell the moment it let go of him. His head was twisted to one side and the deep bite had sheared through most of his neck and upper shoulder. He was dead before his body crumpled to the floor.

As the room fell into silence Lucy crawled out from behind the bar and saw the devastation. She found the fallen forms of Min and Jack. She crawled over to where Jack lay. She fell on him weeping.

Chapter 19 Home

Hector and I stepped out into the early evening air and walked down a slate path to the sidewalk. I looked back at the tall two storey home behind me. It was a very modern home, probably built in the last few years. Even though it didn't, I thought it looked almost exactly like every other home in the area. I guess I wasn't up to my usual analytical view regarding architecture that night.

Hector and I began walking toward the end of the street. As we walked, I called a taxi to pick us up at a gas station I'd located about a mile from us.

The silence seemed to expand as we strolled along the lane. Within 10 minutes we arrived at the station. Hector bought some chips and an offensive looking hot dog while I stood outside and watched people passively filling their tanks.

When the taxi arrived, we were taken to the local hospital. Hector had broken three bones and dislocated several more. Once set and casted, we found a hotel not far from there and got two rooms. We were both exhausted so after deciding to meet at 8:00 am, we went to our separate rooms.

I was asleep in an instant. The dream came quickly. Grieta spoke to me. She was thankful. She seemed to be worried about me.

"I watched you cross into your world and realized you hadn't returned to the original starting point. This bothered me till I realized that I was seeing into the open half of the gate that was the geode. When I turned my mind to the closed gate I realized that an evil being had made its way across."

I sensed that some of these creatures she could slow but others that were either powerful or could exist in either world were not as easy to delay. This one seemed to be able to jump from contact point to contact point without the need to travel through the mind.

"I will show you what I sensed at the other gate." She said.

In my dream I saw a dragon coiled at the bottom of the sea. It was guarding a black pearl that radiated a pure white light. Its coils wound slowly in rhythm to the breath and beat of the sea.

From within the pearl a tiger began to form first as a spot of darkness within the darkness, then as a mist on the shiny surface of the pearl. The reflection then stepped from the pearl and grew to huge proportions. It loomed large over the dragon who recognized it as evil and engaged it in battle.

The dragon's movements were shaped by will and skill and long centuries of practiced discipline. The tiger moved with a rage and anger that seemed unstoppable.

Each in turn hurt the other and the dragon for a moment seemed to subdue the tiger. The tiger then changed its form to that of a winged demon. I recognized this as its true shape. As it changed it healed.

The dragon tried to defeat it before the change could be completed. The demon was too powerful and soon the dragon was close to defeat.

Then a shadow stepped forth from the waters to the south and, using the jeweled dagger that I knew so well, it slew the demon. The demon would not be defeated so easily. In its last dying action it killed the shadow.

I awoke.

As I lay in bed searching for the meaning of the dream, I came to see that a greater battle was being fought. I was not the lone participant in the war against the invaders from the other side.

I realized that the dragon was in fact the next person who took up the challenge. Dragons lived and died without anyone understanding the depth of sacrifice they continued to provide to ensure the safety of a population that hopefully, would never know of the war raging around them.

In the morning, Hector and I got a taxi to my old home. It still had not been cleaned up completely. Though the house was gone, there were the telltale signs that a fire had recently ravaged the lot.

I thought for a moment and decided it was time to try my ability here and see the memory of what happened the last hours of my parents' life. Perhaps I was feeling suddenly nostalgic. Maybe a morbid curiosity came to me. For whatever reason, I uttered those words slowly and clearly.

Then I knew everything. I knew then that my parents had been the guardians of the geode gate. That their attempt to stop a creature from coming over had resulted in it being split many years before I was born. They'd kept the geode from me.

They raised me and trained me to be their successor, to guard the gate and to protect the world from this great calamity. But I'd rebuked their teachings. I rebelled against their dreams for me.

Maybe it was because I felt so little affinity for humanity myself. But that was also part of their plan. They needed me to know I was not like others and not to trust anyone enough to create an emotional bond. The inevitable result was heartache at the death of those you love.

Here I was connecting more now than I ever had, and following a path chosen not by me. Fate, it seemed, did play a part in the lives of men. What else could you call it?

And somehow I'd managed to have possession of both halves of the geode. If that wasn't following a destiny then one must accept that coincidence was certainly working overtime. No, fate was what was working now.

I suppose it was time for me to accept my fate.

The fire had been started during a battle with the spider-headed guy Hector and I'd just destroyed. He said it was a relic from a time when 5 gates were in one place. I saw them all.

The geode, the rift in the basement, the tree branch, the river rock, and the crystal had all been in the possession of the Manandans over four hundred years ago. The battle that was fought was over these relics, these bits of Grieta in our world. There were others of course, but these were all linked in a way I didn't yet understand.

I resolved that my fate must be to bring them back together and find a way to protect them from those that would use them for evil.

I called Maria and told her what I'd uncovered. She didn't seem surprised. She was happy I was ok and gave me an update on Thomas and his current state of development. It seemed that he might make a fine protector of the gate. At his early state he was already starting to speak. The words were almost unintelligible but I think they were Latin. At least that's what I'll tell people when they ask.

Chapter 20 New Sentinels

We returned to Albuquerque by plane. The uneventful flight was, more than anything, an opportunity to get to know Hector better.

He was a bright and amiable man with a ready wit and a clear mind. The more I talked to him, the more I realized how his antics on our first meeting were not only not him, but him, in a way, making fun of himself. You see he never thought he'd amount to much more than being a butcher like his father.

We seemed to be fast friends by the time we'd landed. Our shared trauma and success fueled a lasting friendship that, as my days come close to their end is unshakable.

We were met at the airport by Lucy and Min. As Min drove back to Lucy's home she told of Jack's sacrifice. We wept for her. And we wept because he was an inspiration. He was in the truest sense, a hero. I felt a stinging feeling as I thought of all the work he and I had accomplished in the last several days. I came to think of him as more than a friend.

Family, I guess, like Hector and Min were now family. And Lucy, she would be family.

I thought more about what family means. In all my life I'd only felt close enough to a few to call it that. Although I realized I loved my parents, the mechanics of our family were just that, mechanical.

The Draksons made me feel welcome and needed and now those that were left gave me a sense of belonging and love.

These amazing people gave me a similar feeling of connection. I knew that we would all find it in ourselves to make whatever sacrifice we needed to safeguard each other. And then in fact, we would do our best to safeguard the rest of humanity.

The funeral was on a rare rainy day. Ron had joined us for the burial service and after we retired to Lucy's home for a rosary. I didn't drink much so instead I watched as they slowly filled the empty space left by Jack's absence with drinks. I heard stories from some of his friends on the force who were in attendance.

Lucy sat apart from all of us weeping from time to time. She would occasionally rise to great someone offering her condolences then sit back in the chair she'd claimed and weep again. I resolved not to bother her.

Ron stayed till after everyone but Hector, Min and I'd left.

"I've decided." He said. "I'm going to do my best to help out with your work Chris. Hector and I have been talking with Min. We think it would be best to keep the geodes separate for now. We can protect the one and you the other. That way the enemy can't get at both of them at the same time."

Min added. "I have a lot of knowledge that will help. Like you I was raised to be a Dragon That Guards the Center. Now each of us has a center to keep."

An excerpt from the journal of Jaap Buskirk

The thing had returned. It came to our town and tried to subvert some of the humble souls of our Perish. Our family had been warned and as a result was strong against it. Though there were several deaths few were compelled to join the creatures that corrupted our world.

From survivors we had a description of the thing which temped them. He was a man. On its head was a seam which ran from the crown back to the base of the skull above the line of the neck. This thing was possessed of a great evil. And indeed was still the man who had once been a chief among his own tribe. It was both him and the creature that lived within him.

Those of the tribe that followed it were doomed to eventually become prey to the creatures that devoured the mind. We killed many of them and found in the human head a kind of large parasite.

What it resembled most was a hideous spider with multiple joints in each of its legs. There seemed to be two varieties. One had six limbs the other ten. The best guess is that one was possibly a working drone the other a more intelligent creature.

If true then these things also had the nature of leaders and followers. Perhaps the chief was a higher order of leader for none of the others seemed to have the same disfigurement of the head. What might that creature appear as, is yet to be known to us.

Part of the brain was replaced by some kind of leather spider like thing. Its legs seemed to be made of soft leather jointed every half inch. Each leg was about 6 inches long. At the center is a large mass of soft material that looks like dear antler velvet with small clear tendrils interwoven with the remaining brain.

The upper rear portion of skin was stretched taught. Under the skin, it appeared as though fingers interlocked over a seam that ran from the center of the cranium on top, and slightly offset, to just above the base of the skull. This gave the appearance of a zipper up the back of his head.

There were five creatures. Each shaped loosely like a man. They were tall and thin with deep chests. The long legs had extra joints that bent at an odd backward angle. The long six fingered hands sported wicked looking claws. The heads were triangular. The pointed bottoms and wide tops were slightly curved, creating a domed effect. There were no features in the faces. No noses mouths or eyes to disrupt the dark grey visage. Their legs were anchored in the rock but moving with it, making ripples of stone where they stepped.

It seemed that as each moment passed the creature was healing itself. First the wrist seemed to straighten followed by a snapping sound which indicated its bones had mended. The jaw which had been slack snapped shut. There came a loud popping sound followed by a grinding. A low growl came from its snarling mouth. Its arms stretched wide and seemed to elongate. Its snout pulled back into a short muzzle. The legs twisted into a new, more human, form. In only a few seconds it had transformed into a more simian shape with smaller ears at the side of its head.

Proof

42678908R00124